THEY TOOK THE TRAIL TO TAOS

Jeanne Townsend—A beauty with a taste for intrigue and adventure, she could outthink—and even outfight—most men she met. But she couldn't outrun a bullet, and she couldn't escape the power of love.

Stuart Davis—He had ridden his final trail as a deputy marshal. Could he now stand by and watch innocent people die, or would his sense of justice compel him to reach for his gun?

Lloyd Forrest—A successful gambler, cynical, slick, self-assured. Would he now gamble his life to save the lives of strangers? Or would he coldly fold his hand and walk away?

Darryl Landreth—He was planning the biggest political coup of his life, and no one would stand in his way—not even the gorgeous redhead who had captured his cold heart and knew his darkest secrets.

Matt Briggs—He and his band of hardcases rode for Darryl Landreth, for money and for glory. He didn't much like killing women, but in Jeanne Townsend's case he'd gladly make an exception.

The Stagecoach Series
Ask your bookseller for the books you have missed

STAGECOACH STATION 32:
TAOS

Hank Mitchum

™

Created by the producers of
**Wagons West, White Indian,
Badge, and Winning the West.**

Book Creations Inc., Canaan, NY · Lyle Kenyon Engel, Founder

BANTAM BOOKS
TORONTO · NEW YORK · LONDON · SYDNEY · AUCKLAND

STAGECOACH STATION 32: TAOS

*A Bantam Book / published by arrangement with
Book Creations, Inc.*

Bantam edition / November 1987

*Produced by Book Creations, Inc.
Lyle Kenyon Engel: Founder*

ISBN 0-553-26856-2

Published simultaneously in the United States and Canada

PRINTED IN THE UNITED STATES OF AMERICA

KR   0 9 8 7 6 5 4 3 2 1

STAGECOACH STATION 32:
TAOS

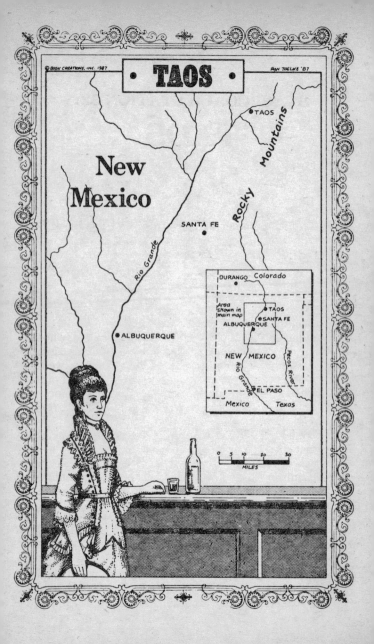

Chapter One

It was a hot summer night in 1881, and the Black Bull was living up to its reputation as the best saloon in Albuquerque, New Mexico. Thick smoke from countless cigars filled the air, mixing with raucous laughter and the tinny notes of a player piano. A woman in a low-cut, spangled costume tried to sing a tender love song, but no one was paying any attention to her except one drunken young ranch hand who gazed at her with cowlike devotion.

Adding to the clamor were the rattle of roulette wheels, the slap of cards, the clinking of whiskey bottles against shot glasses. The room was full of townsmen, as well as miners and ranchers from the surrounding area, all out to enjoy themselves. Fancy-dressed gamblers and women in scanty outfits haunted the tables, eager to help the revelers spend their money.

Crystal chandeliers hung from the ceiling and cast a glow that sparkled brightly on the myriad of bottles along the back of the bar. Above the bottles was a huge gilt-framed mirror flanked by paintings of amply endowed nudes. It was clear that there was no place quite like a saloon for raking in money.

Jeanne Townsend stood at the blackjack table and, as the house dealer, did her part to contribute to the Black Bull's profits. Her long, slender fingers deftly manipulated the deck of cards in her hand.

"And a nine to this gentleman," she said as she flipped a card faceup to one of the men standing around the table. "That's sixteen showing." She arched her carefully plucked red eyebrows and looked at the player, waiting for his decision.

The fellow was a townsman, a storekeeper, well fed but not too prosperous. He had heaved a sigh of relief when the nine of diamonds had turned up, telling Jeanne that he was very close to having the twenty-one that he needed. Everyone else around the table had been eliminated on this hand by going over twenty-one. Now it was between Jeanne and this man. He licked his lips and stared down at the cards in concentration; then he glanced over at the two cards in front of Jeanne, the faceup card being a ten.

He has to have twenty, Jeanne thought, since the man did not immediately say that he was standing pat. He was probably afraid that Jeanne had a ten or a face card hidden, which would also give her a twenty. And a tie went to the dealer. But she did not believe he would risk the odds by drawing again. As if to confirm her instinct, the man said after a pause, "That's enough for me."

He was leaving it up to her, and he smiled when she turned up her hidden card. It was a six, giving her sixteen. Since a dealer had to draw with a hand of sixteen or less, she was required to take another card, and the man knew that the odds were that she would go over.

She smiled sweetly at the man, who was watching her nervously, and turned the next card in the deck, dropping it beside the others.

A sigh went around the table. It was the five of hearts.

"That's twenty-one," Jeanne said. She reached out to gather in the money on the table.

The townsman, who had rolled his eyes heavenward as Jeanne had dealt the winning card, now reached out and put his hand on hers. Jeanne stiffened, fearing that he was going to make trouble over losing.

But instead the man just smiled at her and said, "I must say, ma'am, that losing to a woman as beautiful as yourself is an honor. An honor indeed."

Jeanne returned his smile. It was good to meet a gracious loser for a change. "Stick around," she said lightly. "Maybe your luck will get better."

"I hope so." The message in his eyes was plain as he let his gaze rove over her body.

The smile stayed on Jeanne's face, but the warmth went out of her expression as she pulled her hand away from his. This man was not so different from the others, after all.

She should have been used to the stares, she thought. She had been getting them long enough. Ever since she had turned fourteen, ten years before, men had been looking at her like that. And after all, she *was* working in a saloon. It was not as if she were attending a church social here.

Several feet away, leaning on the bar that ran the length of the room, Darryl Landreth watched Jeanne at work and thought, not for the first time, that she was the most beautiful woman in a whole roomful of pretty women. He took in the rich sweep of her luxuriant red curls, pinned up now on her head in an intricate arrangement, admired her fair skin and more-than-pleasing features, swept his eyes over the full, ripe curves of her body in the tight green silk dress. It was cut low at the bosom so that the white swells of her breasts tantalized the customers and kept them happy even while they were losing their hard-earned money to her.

Hiring Jeanne to deal blackjack was one of the best decisions he had made lately, Landreth reflected. The woman had a great deal of potential. Later, when he had cleared up some business dealings, he just might find out how much potential she really had.

At the moment there were other things on Landreth's mind. Owning and operating the Black Bull was time-consuming enough. He had other interests, too, that demanded his attention.

Darryl Landreth looked like a prosperous business-man. His dark suit was given a slightly more dashing air by the frills of his snow-white shirt and the diamond stickpin in his cravat. Another jewel glittered in the heavy gold ring on his right hand. He had a cigar clamped between even white teeth. His carefully barbered hair was dark, with not a hint of gray, as was the full mustache over his wide, expressive mouth. He was a handsome man, no doubt of that.

And there was not a single crooked deal in this town that he did not have his finger in, a fact on which he prided himself.

Jeanne felt someone watching her and glanced around to see her employer leaning on the bar and looking her way. Their eyes met for a brief moment. Landreth took the cigar out of his mouth, nodded, and smiled at her. Jeanne returned the smile before turning her attention back to the play around the table. She blushed slightly, a fact made more noticeable by her fair skin. The admiration with which Landreth was regarding her was obvious. He was interested in her, she could tell, and sooner or later he would act on that interest. Jeanne was counting on that, though she knew full well just what kind of man Darryl Landreth was. That was why she was here in Albuquerque in the first place.

A new player was stepping up to the table, she saw as she refocused her attention on the game. He wore range clothes, but the arrogant expression on his young face and the way his pistol rode in its low-slung holster told her that he was more than a simple cowhand. He was a gunslinger, or at least he fancied himself to be one. The grin he gave her and the way he ran his gaze over her body said he was a ladies' man, too. Instinct told Jeanne that he also might be trouble.

Over the next few hands, Jeanne got a pretty good idea of how he played. Not surprisingly, his game was impatient and daring, and more often than not he went over twenty-one on his cards and was eliminated from the game. When he did win, the hand was usually a good one for him, but an occasional win could not offset his steady losses. Gradually, the cocky smile left his face and was replaced by a taut look of concentration.

As Jeanne dealt, his eyes never left her swiftly moving fingers. She did not mind that he was watching her closely. She dealt an honest game, and she had made a point of telling Landreth exactly that when she had asked him for the job a week earlier. He had chuckled and told her that whatever she wanted to do was fine with him.

Maybe he liked the idea of having one honest game in the Black Bull; it made a nice change of pace for the saloon. So the young cowboy could watch all he wanted, she thought. He was not going to catch her cheating.

"Blackjack," she said, turning over a queen to go with the ace she already had. "Too bad, gents."

"Yeah," the cowboy said. "Just too damn bad, ain't it, lady?"

Jeanne curbed the anger she felt at his harsh tone. She forced a bright smile and said, "I'm sure your luck will turn around, mister."

"It'd damn well better," the cowboy growled in reply, his meaning evident to the players gathered around the table.

One of the players, a middle-aged man in a battered black hat, said, "No call for talk like that, friend. Nobody's makin' you play."

The cowboy glared at him and let his right hand drop down to brush against the butt of his Colt. "You just stay out of it, old-timer. I know what I'm doin'."

For a moment the older man looked as if he were going to take offense and carry the argument further, but something about the young cowboy's coiled-spring stance made him think better of it. He swallowed, ran a hand over his grizzled jaw, and muttered, "Just don't like folks talkin' that way to ladies."

"It's all right," Jeanne told the older man softly. "I'm sure the *gentleman* didn't mean anything by what he said."

The tart emphasis was not lost on the cowboy, who flushed angrily and said, "I meant what I meant. Just deal the cards."

Jeanne dealt, and as luck would have it, the hand came down to the cowboy, the middle-aged man, and herself. Though the merriment in the rest of the saloon went on at the same level, it became quiet around the blackjack table.

Jeanne kept smiling, even though she felt the tension gnawing on her nerves. "Would you care for a card?" she asked the middle-aged man, holding the deck ready and in plain sight.

The man had a ten showing. He lifted the corner of his hidden card one more time, checked it, and then nodded to Jeanne, who dealt the next card.

Another ten, making a twenty showing, which meant the hidden card would put him over twenty-one. The man grimaced when he saw the ten, and then he shrugged and grinned sheepishly. "Reckon it's not my night," he said.

Jeanne's gaze moved on to the cowboy, who was watching her intently. "What about you?" she asked.

He did not look down at his cards. He had a seven showing. Jeanne guessed he would want at least one more card.

"All right," he said sharply.

She flipped the card out in front of him. His eyes darted down to it and recognized it as the five of spades.

The cowboy took a deep breath and blew it out. "One more," he said.

Jeanne hesitated. He had twelve showing, and she knew damn well that another card would likely put him over. His hidden card must be very low, she mused, which was why he was plunging ahead.

"What are you waitin' for?" he asked, harshly and abruptly. "Deal the damned card!"

She dealt him the jack of hearts—making twenty-two showing—and saw the color go out of his face.

His hand shot out and grabbed her wrist, squeezing hard and making her drop the deck. The cards scattered over the table as he jerked her toward him. "You little bitch!" he blazed. "You been cheatin', ain't you? Admit it!"

She could smell the raw whiskey on his breath and knew he was out of control, swept away by the liquor and his anger. Over his shoulder, she could see a couple of Darryl Landreth's bouncers pushing through the crowd. They were big men, burly and brutal, and she knew they would beat the young cowboy to a pulp if given the chance.

Landreth himself had left the bar and was hurrying toward the disturbance, his hand hovering just inside the flap of his coat. He carried a derringer there; Jeanne had caught a glimpse of it several times. If she did not put a stop to this herself, there was going to be a lot of trouble, more trouble than she wanted.

The cowboy was still yanking on her wrist and cursing, so she stopped resisting and let herself be pulled up against him. The sudden movement caught him by surprise and threw him somewhat off-balance. It was then that Jeanne brought her knee up, swift and hard.

The cowboy let out a howl and staggered back, clutching futilely at the injured area. Jeanne clenched her fist and brought it around with perfect timing, putting all her weight and deceptive strength behind the blow. The punch caught the cowboy on the point of the chin and snapped his head around. He went to one knee, glassy-eyed.

Jeanne ignored the pain she felt in her right hand and, stepping behind the cowboy, reached down with her left and plucked his gun out of its holster. He must have felt her taking the pistol, for he came out of his stupor with a shake of his head and a bull-like roar of pain and anger. Without flinching, she stepped back and squeezed the trigger.

The Colt blasted and bucked against her palm, the slug plowing into the floor between the cowboy's feet and sending splinters flying. He gave an involuntary hop and then froze, staring down the barrel of his own gun.

"I don't take kindly to being roughed up or called a cheater, mister," Jeanne told him in a cold voice.

"B-be careful, lady," the cowboy said nervously. "That thing could go off again."

"That's right. And it's going to be pointed at you the next time." She decided to let him think that the first shot was an accident. That would worry him more than telling him she was a crack shot with more different kinds of guns than he had ever seen. "Now, I think an apology is in order," she went on.

Landreth and his bouncers had stopped and were watching the show, like everyone else in the big room. There was a wide grin on Landreth's face as he saw how well his beautiful new blackjack dealer was acquitting herself.

"I . . . I reckon I'm sorry, ma'am," the cowboy stammered. "I didn't mean no harm."

"Do you still think I was cheating?" Jeanne demanded.

"No, ma'am. You won fair and square."

"I won because you're reckless, cowboy," she said a little more softly now. "I think you'd better get out of here."

He summoned up enough courage to gesture at the pistol and ask. "What about my gun?"

"Come back and get it tomorrow. I'll leave it with the bartender. Now, are you going?"

"Yeah, I'm goin'." He turned and walked stiffly from the saloon to a chorus of laughter and catcalls. The look he gave Jeanne over his shoulder was a mixture of frustration and anger. Then he pushed through the swinging doors and disappeared into the night.

"I want to talk to you, Jeanne," Landreth said from beside her. He motioned to one of the house men. "Let Hugh take over your table for a while."

She nodded. "All right." She thought for a moment that he was angry with her for letting the scene take place, since he was no longer grinning, but then she saw the corners of his mouth curling and knew that he was holding in a smile.

She gave the cowboy's pistol to one of the waiters and told him to leave it with the bartender. Then she followed Landreth through the crowd to his personal table in a secluded corner of the room. As she passed among the customers, she was aware of the grins they were giving her. A few even offered their congratulations on the way she had handled the cowboy.

Landreth held a chair for her at his table and then motioned to the bartender to send over a bottle and glasses. As he settled down in his chair across the table, he smiled and said, "Would you like a drink?"

"I think that's a good idea." She summoned a weak smile, realizing that he might think the experience she had just gone through should have shaken her up more than it had. She did not want to do anything to make Landreth suspicious.

One of the waiters brought a bottle of brandy and a couple of snifters on a silver tray. As Landreth poured the liquor for both of them, he chuckled. "Well, Jeanne, you handled that trouble as well as any of my bouncers." He handed her one of the snifters. "You're much lovelier, though."

"Thank you." Jeanne sipped the brandy gratefully, feeling the warmth of it spreading through her. "I really wasn't trying to cause a commotion. I just got upset when that brute tried to manhandle me and accused me of cheating. You know I run an honest game."

"Yes, indeed. And don't worry about causing a scene. The customers loved the show." He leaned back in his chair. "Maybe I should make it a regular part of the evening's entertainment."

Jeanne smiled and shook her head. "No, thank you, Mr. Landreth. I don't believe I'd be interested."

"You've been working for me for a week now, Jeanne. Don't you think it's time you started calling me Darryl?"

The question did not surprise Jeanne. She had been waiting for just such an opening gambit. She took another sip of her brandy to cover her hesitation and then said slowly, "All right . . . Darryl."

Landreth took a drink and considered the beautiful woman across the table. She seemed almost shy now, but she certainly had not looked demure with a Colt in her hand and fire in her eyes. For a moment he wondered where such a young woman had learned to handle herself so well, but then he dismissed the question. She had worked in other saloons; that much was obvious from the way she handled cards. Any saloon girl soon learned to take care of herself.

From the first instant Jeanne had entered his saloon, Landreth had wanted her. He had taken things a little slowly, though, sensing that Jeanne was different from the other women who worked at the Black Bull. During the time she had been here, she had not teased him, had not led him on, but on the other hand, she had not done anything to make him think she was opposed to a more intimate relationship.

"You're a damn good blackjack dealer, Jeanne," he finally said. "But I think you're cut out for more important things."

"I am?" she replied, somewhat surprised.

"Yes." He nodded firmly. "I'm convinced of it. How would you feel about coming up to my suite a little later so that we can discuss the, ah, possibilities?"

Good Lord, Jeanne thought. *How naive does he think I am?*

She carefully kept that thought from showing on her face. She could see how his charm would probably work on most women in this business. She was not like most women, however, and for that matter she was not in this business: Jeanne was an agent for the Pinkerton Detective Agency, working under cover to learn of Landreth's dirty dealings. The family of one of Landreth's victims—for whose murder Landreth had been acquitted on a legal technicality—had hired the agency in hopes that the murderer would be imprisoned on other charges.

"Of course," she said sweetly. "I think I'd enjoy that very much." She cast her eyes down toward the table, playing the not-quite innocent. There was no doubt in her mind about the answer she had given. A man like Landreth would not be above firing a woman who refused to go along with his advances. And she could not afford to be fired now—not before she had the incriminating evidence that she had come to Albuquerque to get.

Landreth was smiling, pleased that she had agreed to visit his suite on the saloon's upper floor. Then his expression became serious as someone caught his eye. He said to Jeanne, "Why don't you stay here, my dear, and have some more of this excellent brandy? I have to go take care of some business."

Jeanne watched as Landreth got up from the table and made his way across the room. When he reached the bar, he paused beside a man who was standing there drinking whiskey. This newcomer was tall, lean, and muscular, with sandy hair under his pushed-back brown Stetson. As Landreth spoke to him, the man tossed back a shot of whiskey and banged the glass down on the mahogany bar for a refill.

Jeanne recognized the man. His name was Matt Briggs, and he was an outlaw. There were rumors that he led a gang that had committed robberies all over New Mexico Territory. No one had been able to prove his guilt, so there were no reward posters circulating on him and he could ride freely wherever he wanted. Jeanne had seen him several times in the Black Bull, and each time Landreth had something to say to him. She was almost sure that Matt Briggs worked for Landreth—that Landreth was the real brains behind Briggs's gang.

Landreth and Briggs were talking in low but animated tones, and Jeanne wished that she had mastered the skill of reading lips. Still, she could guess that Landreth was going to be busy for a while.

Sensing an opportunity waiting to be seized, Jeanne finished her drink and stood up, moving away from Landreth's private table and blending in with the crowd as she went toward the staircase at the back of the room.

She kept an eye on Landreth and Briggs as she made her way up the stairs, but neither of the men so much as glanced her way. Traffic on the stairs was not unusual, since Landreth did not care what the women did in their rooms so long as he got a cut of the proceeds. When she reached the upper floor landing, Jeanne turned left instead of right, away from the tiny rooms where the women lived.

The hallway in this direction was short, and at the end of it was the door leading into Landreth's suite. Jeanne had never been there, but from talking to some of the women who had, she knew its layout. There was a sitting room with a small office to one side, and beyond the sitting room was Landreth's bedchamber.

Jeanne paused before the door, reaching down gingerly to try the knob. It was locked, as she had expected. She glanced down the hall to confirm that no one else was there, then reached up and plucked a long pin from her hair, ignoring the now-unpinned curl that tumbled down the back of her neck. Realizing she had no way of knowing how long her luck would last, she bent to the task, frowning in concentration as she worked the pin into the lock.

Less than a minute later, she heard the click that told her she had been successful. She straightened, opened the door, and stepped inside the sitting room, quickly closing the door behind her. She could not relock it; she would have needed the key for that. But she hoped to be in and out before anyone noticed that she was gone from downstairs.

Jeanne had been prepared for this chance. She took a short, stubby candle and a packet of matches from a concealed pocket of her dress. A moment later she had the candle lit, its flame casting a soft, flickering glow over the room.

Jeanne went to the door of Landreth's office and found it unlocked. Grateful for the extra time that gave her, she slipped into the little windowless room and closed the door behind her. Then she went to the desk, which took up most of the space. There was a heavy brass smoking stand next to the desk, and she set the candle on top of it.

Moving with efficient speed, Jeanne began to search the desk. She started with the large middle drawer and then proceeded to the drawers on the side. Most of what she found was paperwork relating to the running of the Black Bull, but there were a few other documents—most of them letters—that looked interesting. She did not take the time to read them but instead simply concealed them inside the bosom of her dress. There would be time enough later to study them and see if they were what she was looking for.

In the last drawer, the bottom one on the right-hand side, she found Landreth's cashbox. It was locked, but the fastener was a flimsy one; she knew she could have it open in a matter of seconds. If there was time, she would open the box and take some of the money before she left the office so that Landreth would think he had been the victim of a common thief.

Of much more interest to her was the leather-bound book that was sitting on top of the cashbox. She picked it up and rapidly flipped through its pages, feeling her pulse quicken as she saw the columns of names, dates, and dollar amounts scrawled there. She would need time to analyze them, but judging from the names listed, the book could prove to be exactly what she needed: a record of Darryl Landreth's crooked transactions.

She gasped and jerked her head up as the door to the sitting room suddenly burst open. Landreth stood there, his eyes blazing with anger, and Jeanne had time only for one silent, heartfelt curse before he reached across the desk and slapped the book out of her hands.

Jeanne gave a cry of surprise as Landreth exclaimed, "I hate a goddamned sneak thief! What are you doing up here?"

Jeanne's brain was working furiously. Part of it was castigating herself for not hearing Landreth coming into the suite because she had been so absorbed in what she had found in the record book. Another part was searching desperately for a way out of this.

"Why . . . why, you told me you wanted me to come up here!" she said, trying to play the innocent victim.

"I said later, not now," Landreth grated. He glanced over his shoulder, and Jeanne noticed for the first time that one of the barmen was with him. "Wait out in the hall for me, Joe." He swung back to Jeanne. "Now, what the hell were you doing, going through my desk?"

"I was just waiting for you, and I got bored." She let her expression go pouty. "I didn't steal anything, if that's what you're worried about."

For a moment she thought her pose was going to work. Doubt and confusion mixed with the anger on Landreth's face. But then his features hardened, and he said softly, "Oh, no, you little witch, you're not going to put anything over on me. You had a reason for being here, and I'm going to find out what it is!"

He strode around the desk and grabbed her arm, shaking her roughly. Jeanne began to cry, again protesting her innocence. She already knew, however, that she might have to fight her way out of here, and Landreth was no drunken young cowboy to be taken by surprise.

"Mr. Landreth . . ." The tentative voice came from the doorway. Joe, the barman, stood there, clearly uncomfortable. "Mr. Landreth, Briggs said that he's in a hurry. . . ."

Landreth caught himself and stopped shaking Jeanne. He took a deep breath to compose himself and then said, "You're right. You stay there in the sitting room and watch the door, Joe. I'm going to leave this thieving tramp here, but I'll be back for her later." There was an ominous promise in his voice.

Landreth took the cashbox with him and stalked out,

obviously heading downstairs to pay off Briggs for some
illegal errand. Jeanne took a step toward the door of the
office, but Joe shut it solidly, and she heard him dragging
a chair over to sit in front of it.

In the flickering candlelight, Jeanne looked around
the windowless room. She was trapped, all right. She had
thought when she had come up to Landreth's suite that
the saloon owner would be tied up with Briggs for longer
than he had been. Obviously, she had figured wrong.

The tears she had been crying had stopped as soon as
Landreth left the room; there was no point in them now.
Jeanne sighed and shook her head, disgusted with herself
for letting Landreth catch her. She should have known
better than to make a mistake like that.

It was the kind of mistake that might wind up getting
her killed.

Chapter Two

As Jeanne Townsend stood in Darryl Landreth's room, she knew she could not afford to dwell on her mistake. The little time she had while Landreth was downstairs could be put to a better use, such as coming up with a way out of this messy situation.

She looked around the office. There was no window, and the only way in or out was through the door to the sitting room. She could hear the occasional scrape of the chair as Joe shifted around on the other side of the door.

Stepping closer to the door, Jeanne raised her voice and called through it, "I could sure use a drink." If she could lure the barman in here, she was certain she could handle him.

Joe laughed, a harsh, unsympathetic sound. "So could I, if I was in as much trouble as you, lady," he replied.

Jeanne grimaced. He was more interested in staying on Landreth's good side than he was in playing up to her. She supposed she could not blame him for that.

She shook her head and looked around again. Besides the desk and the chair and the smoking stand, the only other piece of furniture in the room sat next to the wall—a bureau with attached mirror. She stared into the mirror for a long moment and then hurried to the desk, where she bent to pick up the smoking stand. Placing the burning candle on the desk, she hefted the stand. She realized it would take effort to swing it around and use it as a weapon, but she knew she was strong enough to do it.

She moved over beside the bureau and set the stand

down. Then, using the wall to brace herself, she slipped
her fingers behind the bureau and shoved it away from the
wall enough so that she could put her shoulder against it.
She held the bottom in place with a foot while pushing
against the top of it until the heavy bureau tipped forward,
crashing to the floor. The mirror shattered, sending shards
of glass all over the carpet. Lifting the heavy smoking
stand, she positioned herself beside the door and waited.

Suddenly the door popped open and Joe rushed
through, his eyes wide to see what had made the crash.
He tried to stop when he saw the overturned bureau in
front of him, but his momentum was too great. His shins
cracked into the heavy piece of furniture, and he let out a
yelp of pain. The cry was cut off by a thud as Jeanne hit
him in the head with the smoking stand. Joe staggered,
his eyes rolling up in his head, and fell. He let out a groan
and then lay still.

Jeanne knelt beside him and was relieved to find a
strong pulse in his throat. She had tried not to hit him
hard enough to kill him, but in such a desperate situation
she could not take the time to be too careful. She undid
his belt, yanked it loose, and then used it to tie his hands
behind his back. A strip of cloth torn from the hem of her
dress served as a gag.

When she stood a few seconds later, she was confident that Joe would not be raising an alarm for several
minutes. Someone downstairs could have heard the crash
when the bureau fell over, however, so she had to hurry.

Landreth had taken the record book with him, so she
would have to abandon any hope of getting her hands on
it. She still had the letters she had hidden in her dress,
and though she was not sure what significance they might
have, she did recognize that one of the authors had been
involved in questionable activities in the past. She would
have to be satisfied with them. For the time being, her
main worry was getting out of the Black Bull with her life.
Once she was away from here, she would drop the name
she had been using under cover—Jeanne Fontanne—and
change her appearance.

When she stepped out into the hall, she could hear
the music and laughter coming from downstairs. The vol-

ume of noise did not seem to have lessened any, so
perhaps the sounds from the office had gone unnoticed.
Jeanne bit her lip, hesitated for an instant, and then
turned toward a window that opened out into the alley
behind the saloon. She was not even going to return to
her room for the rest of her things; nothing there was
worth her life.

Suddenly she heard Landreth's voice. The words grew
louder, and she knew he was coming up the stairs. Her
fingers clawed at the window, sliding it up. It was stubborn, but Jeanne got it raised enough to duck down and
slip through the opening. Holding on to the sill, she
looked up and saw the rain gutter running along the edge
of the roof a few feet above the window.

She pulled herself up, balancing precariously on the
windowsill, reaching up toward the gutter. Her fingertips
brushed it. She extended a little farther, getting all the
reach she could, and clamped a grip on the metal gutter.

Holding her breath, she swung out away from the
window. Her other hand found a grip, and she edged
away from the window to the right, her weight pulling
painfully at her shoulder joints. Luckily the corner of the
building was only a few feet from her; there the gutter
turned downward to form a vertical rain spout. In spite of
her long dress, which hampered her somewhat, she was
able to wrap her legs around the spout and shimmy down.
When she was still five feet from the ground, she heard
shouting from the second floor and knew that Landreth
had discovered the trussed-up barman.

Jeanne kicked off her high-heeled shoes and let go of
the rain spout, falling to the ground. She lost her balance
when she landed, sat down hard, but then scrambled to
her feet. With one hand she rubbed her bruised bottom,
and with the other she gathered up the shoes.

She glanced up at the open window above her head
and saw movement there. Hugging the wall to stay out of
sight as much as possible, she started to run. She knew,
all too well, that she was running for her life.

Darryl Landreth knelt beside Joe and used his pocket
knife to cut the belt binding the barman's hands. Landreth's
face was contorted with anger, and he was none too care-

ful as he sawed at the leather. The blade nicked Joe's
wrist, starting a small trickle of blood, but the barman did
not say a word. He was worried that Landreth would do
even worse after the way he had botched things up.

"What happened?" Landreth asked in a low voice as
he took the gag out of Joe's mouth.

"I heard a loud noise and came in to see what had
happened," Joe said shakily. "I tripped over the bureau,
and then the lady clouted me." His hands were free now,
and he lifted one of them to touch gingerly the sore-
looking knot that had sprung up on his head.

Matt Briggs stuck his head in the door of Landreth's
room and took in the scene. He had heard Landreth's
shout upon the discovery of the woman's escape and had
hurried upstairs. "What the hell happened here?" he asked.

Landreth swung toward him. "Go downstairs and get
some of the boys," he rasped. "I want you to find
somebody."

"Sure. Who are we looking for?"

"One of the girls who works here—Jeanne Fontanne—
that pretty redheaded blackjack dealer I hired a week
ago." His tone became more savage. "I caught her in here
rifling my desk. She got away from Joe here."

The barman, who was hauling himself to his feet,
gulped slightly as he heard the anger in Landreth's voice.
Ignoring the throbbing in his head, he said, "I'll help look
for her, boss," and hurried past Briggs out the door.

Landreth glared after him for a second and then
shook his head. He had more important things to worry
about. "You'd better get started," he said to Briggs. "It's
worth fifty dollars to the man who brings her in."

The gunman nodded. "We'll find her."

From the hall, Joe suddenly called, "There she goes!"

Landreth and Briggs sprang to the doorway and saw
the barman peering out through an open window. Briggs
glanced at Landreth and then hurried away to gather his
men and get the pursuit started.

Landreth returned to the office, stepped around the
debris of the mirror, and settled himself in the thickly
padded leather swivel chair behind the desk. The candle
that Jeanne had been using for illumination was still sput-

tering on the desktop, and Landreth blew it out after
lighting the kerosene lamp.

He started going through the drawers of the desk,
trying to determine just what the woman had been after.
Her goal had probably been the money. All saloon girls
were thieves at heart, he thought. He riffled through the
bills in the box, which he had brought back with him, and
decided that none of them were missing except for what
he had taken out earlier to pay off Matt Briggs for his
share in a recent stage holdup. He took his record book
from the pocket where he had placed it and dropped it on
top of the box; then he continued his inventory of the
drawers.

A fine sheen of sweat sprang out on his forehead.
Some of the letters were missing, letters that hinted at
specific illegal activities in the past—and alluded to some
that were yet to take place. Jeanne Fontanne was the only
person who could have taken them.

Landreth cursed under his breath as he searched the
other drawers and determined that the papers were indeed gone and not just misplaced. What interest would a
common saloon girl have in such things? Unless Jeanne
Fontanne was not a common saloon girl. . . .

Briggs'll find her, Landreth told himself as he rested
his palms on the desktop and tried to control his emotions.
*He has to find her, and when he does . . . Jean Fontanne
has to die!*

Jeanne paused in the deep shadows of an alley to
catch her breath and try to figure out what her next move
should be. She could not stay in Albuquerque, she was
sure of that. With all his connections in criminal circles,
Darryl Landreth would be able to find her with little
trouble if she tried to hide out.

Her best bet was to get out of town that very night,
before Landreth had time to gather his loose-knit organization and start looking for her in earnest.

Jeanne delved once more into the hidden pocket in
the folds of her dress and pulled out a small roll of bills.
She always carried some money with her; there was never
any way of knowing when she would need it. She slipped

over to the end of the alley and looked out at the street. There were still quite a few lights on, and though Jeanne did not know the town well, she thought she knew where she was.

The railroad station should be about four blocks north of here on the same street, she thought. There were too many people around for her to risk walking boldly down the boardwalk in front of the stores. She would have to keep to the back alleys and the shadows.

She hurried as much as possible, though she had to be careful not to trip over any of the garbage that cluttered the alleys. She did not want any ruckus drawing attention to her.

Before she had arrived in Albuquerque, Jeanne had studied the railroad schedule and knew that an eastbound train was supposed to be pulling out of the station at nine o'clock. Though she did not know the exact time, since her watch was with the rest of her things back in her room at the saloon, it had to be close to nine now. If she missed the train, she did not know what she would do. There was a stage line that left Albuquerque and ran north to Santa Fe and Taos and beyond, but there would not be any stage leaving until the next morning. By then, it would probably be too late.

There was always a chance Landreth had not yet discovered that some of his letters were missing. If that was the case, then he would still think that she was a simple thief, and maybe he would not look for her with the deadly intensity that he would if he suspected the truth. The papers occasionally crinkled against her skin as she strode quickly along, and she hoped they were worth the risks she was running for them.

Jeanne stopped in the gloom of a recessed doorway less than a block from the depot and studied the solid red-brick railway building. There were a few people going in and out, and she felt a surge of relief when she saw that a locomotive and its trailing cars were still sitting on the tracks beyond the station. The nine o'clock train had not left yet. She could buy a ticket and head out of there— perhaps make her way back to Denver to the Pinkerton office.

Of course, regardless of what she did to conceal her identity, she would leave something of a trail behind her. Anyone would remember a redheaded woman, especially one in a green saloon dress, which she would have to wear until it was safe to find other, less conspicuous clothing. Landreth would be able to track her. But by that time, it should not matter, since she would be speeding toward safety on the train. At least, she hoped she would be.

Jeanne started to step out of the doorway when she heard the rapid patter of hurrying hoofbeats. She pulled back into the shadows as three men rode hard up the street and pulled their mounts to a halt outside the depot. As they swung out of their saddles, the light from the lamps on the sidewalk outside the depot washed over their faces, and Jeanne felt a shock of recognition. They were Matt Briggs's men. She had seen them in the saloon with him several times before, and there was no question in her mind about their identities. She had trained herself to remember faces.

One of the men stayed outside while the other two went into the station. They were looking for her, no doubt. Landreth had known that she would try to get out of town. Had he discovered that she had taken the papers? Jeanne could not be sure about that, but she knew it was possible. One thing was now certain: With Briggs's men watching the station, she could not risk leaving Albuquerque by train.

Maybe it was a soft footstep that warned her, or simply some instinct that made her whirl around as a shadowy figure lunged toward her. Jeanne ducked to the side, eluding the man's charge, and she ran down the side of the building toward the alley again. Her heart pounded wildly in her chest, but she told herself to stay calm and not let her panic run away with her. That was the only way she would get out of this town alive.

She heard the man's footsteps pounding behind her in the alley and expected that at any second he would call out to Briggs's men at the depot. But he did not yell, and the only sounds were the footsteps and the harsh, rapid breathing of both of them. He was closing in on her as she darted through the alleyway, heedless now of knocking things over and raising a noise. She could not outrun him, she realized. She was going to have to stand and fight.

Suddenly he was right behind her, reaching out for her. Jeanne swerved to the side as his fingers brushed the back of her dress, gripping the gown for a second and then slipping away. She spun around to face him, her eyes searching the gloom desperately for any sort of weapon.

The man stopped as Jeanne turned toward him, and he stood ready to move either way if she tried to leap past him again. He was breathing heavily, betraying the fact that he was a townsman and out of shape. In the faint light from the stars, Jeanne recognized him as one of the dealers from the Black Bull.

"Dammit, you ran me a good race, girl," he said roughly. "Why don't you just come on back to the saloon with me? Nobody's going to hurt you."

"How much is Landreth offering for me?" Jeanne asked, trying to stall for time. They were in the back lot of one of the town's businesses, and some strange shapes were propped on wooden sawhorses surrounding them. She could smell sawdust and the unmistakable aroma of cut wood.

"Fifty dollars," the man answered. "And I intend to have it."

That was why the man had not called for help earlier, Jeanne realized. He did not want to have to split the reward Landreth was offering. The fact that the reward was only fifty dollars did not mean much; even if he had already discovered the true nature of her theft, he would not want to put too big a price on her head, since it might tempt some to try for more money after they had captured her.

Those thoughts raced through Jeanne's brain—the part of it that was trained for thinking out such things. On a more immediate level, she had recognized what the shadowy shapes on the sawhorses were. Coffins. They were in the back lot of the local undertaking establishment.

Appropriate, Jeanne thought grimly.

And then the man lunged at her again, tired of waiting. She dodged, but his fingers grabbed her arm and sank cruelly into the soft flesh. Biting back the cry of pain that sprang to her lips, Jeanne reached out with her free hand. Her fingers brushed rough wood and closed on it. Snatching up the short two-by-four that was leaning against a half-completed coffin, she whipped the makeshift weapon around in a wicked arc. All of her strength was behind the blow, and the wood slammed against her attacker's head with a sickening crunch.

The man's hold on Jeanne's other arm fell away as he staggered, his hands lifting to his skull. And then he reeled and pitched forward on his face, his sprawled body motionless on the ground.

Jeanne dropped the club, and her knees went suddenly weak as she felt for his pulse and then realized that she had killed him. She had been in trouble plenty of times before and had been forced to use violence, much as she had done with Joe and the young cowboy earlier in the night. But never, until this moment, had she ended another person's life.

A spasm shook her body, and she felt the drinks she had had earlier coming up, along with the rest of what was in her roiling stomach. She stumbled over to one of the sawhorses and leaned on it for long moments until the nausea went away. Then she straightened, shook her head to clear some of the cobwebs, and walked as firmly as she could away from there.

Jeanne was still in deep trouble, and she knew she was the only one who could get herself out of it. Since the train was no longer a possibility, she would have to get out of Albuquerque some other way. If she tried leaving on foot, Landreth's men would have her rounded up by morning, she was sure. There had to be something else.

She continued down the alley away from the undertaker's, weariness gripping her. Passing behind an empty building that had once been a store, she spotted a door leading into the cellar. A thoughtful frown creased her forehead. Landreth would be sure that she would try to leave Albuquerque tonight, and his efforts would be concentrated on keeping her from doing that. If she could hide out for a day or so . . .

She lifted the door to the cellar, grateful that it was not locked, and hesitated only a moment before starting down the stairs into the darkness. When she had pulled the door closed behind her, she chanced striking one of the matches from the packet she had put in her pocket when she dressed. The brief glow showed her a dirty, empty cellar with a low ceiling. She had been afraid that there would be snakes or rats, but there was no sign of any vermin.

It was not much of a hideout, but it would have to do. The night would be long, cold, and hungry, but by the next night, Jeanne thought, she would be able to sneak out of Albuquerque. That is, if she was not found before then.

When the match went out, the darkness was complete, but she did not want to risk detection by lighting another match. There were gaps around the door, and any light shining through them might draw attention. And so she huddled in a corner of the cellar and resigned herself to spending a miserable night. It was not until dawn, with faint gray light filtering into the cellar, that she finally dozed off.

When Jeanne awoke, the whole day had passed and the light outside was rapidly fading. The smell of food cooking in surrounding buildings made her think it was nearing the dinner hour. The painful stiffness she felt in her muscles confirmed her guess that she had slept for more than twelve hours. Knowing that leaving the basement before it was fully dark would be inviting trouble, she settled back to wait.

A little while later, when night had completely darkened the cracks around the door, Jeanne decided it was time to leave. When she had stretched out some of the aches, she carefully went up the stairs and lifted the door that led into the dark alley. There seemed to be no one around, so she stepped out. The night was quiet, with the only sounds coming from the saloons several blocks away. Jeanne grimaced as the thought of the saloons reminded her of Landreth. He had to be going crazy by now, knowing that she was still on the loose with his letters.

Jeanne put her hand inside her dress and felt to make sure the stolen letters were still there. She still had not had a chance to read them, but that would have to wait until she was safely out of Albuquerque.

Her mouth was dry and her stomach was growling with hunger. She took care of her thirst at a rain barrel, despite the fact that the water was brackish. Her hunger, like everything else, could be taken care of when she had put this town safely behind her.

The creak of wheels caught her attention and made her turn her head toward the street. A wagon was passing by, full of cowhands on their way back to their ranch after a day spent carousing, to judge by their laughter and off-key singing.

Jeanne paused in the mouth of the alley and watched the wagon roll toward her, pulled by four mules. She looked around. She was on the edge of town, with only one more building on this side of the street and with the wagon the only vehicle on this stretch of the road. Jeanne took a deep breath and stepped out of the shadows, striding into the street in front of the wagon.

The driver hauled back on the reins, his eyes widening in surprise as he took in Jeanne's attractive form. The mules came to a stop, and she hurried up next to the driver's seat, being careful not to spook the animals and start them kicking.

"Could I hitch a ride with you?" Jeanne asked quickly.

The cowboys riding in the back of the wagon fell silent at the sound of her voice. They twisted their heads around to see what she looked like, peering drunkenly at her in the night.

The driver frowned. "Why, ma'am, you don't even know where we're headed. Don't think it'd be fittin' for a lady to ride with a bunch of cowpokes, anyway."

"I don't care where you're going," Jeanne told him earnestly. "Just as long as it's out of Albuquerque."

The man's frown deepened as he asked, "Are you in some kind of trouble, ma'am?"

"Yes," Jeanne said. "Yes, I am. You see, there's this man . . . he made advances . . ." She let her voice trail off, knowing that she would not have to say any more to get their imaginations working. Despite a rough exterior,

a cowboy was often a romantic creature, Jeanne had found,
eager to see things in melodramatic terms.

The driver shook his head and rubbed his grizzled
jaw. "I don't know, I just don't know. . . ."

"Aw, hell, Luther, give the little lady a ride," one of
the cowboys suddenly spoke up, a Texas twang in his
voice. "Can't you see she needs our help, you ol' buffalo?"

"Who you callin' a buffalo, Gil?" The driver, an older
man, turned back to Jeanne and jerked a thumb over his
shoulder at the bed of the wagon. "Climb aboard, ma'am,"
he said to her. "That is, if you don't mind associatin' with
that pack of cutthroats. I just do their cookin' for them, so
don't confuse me with them."

Jeanne did feel slightly nervous as she climbed into
the wagon, taking the hand of the young man who had
spoken up for her. "I don't mind," she said. "I'm sure
they're all perfect gentlemen."

"Downright little lambs, that's us," the young man
named Gil said with a grin.

As the driver flapped the reins at the backs of the
mules and got the stubborn creatures in motion again,
Jeanne felt relief flooding through her. In a few minutes
they would be leaving Albuquerque behind.

There were no benches around the inside of the
wagon, just the side walls that rose about a foot above the
level of the bed. The wagon bed itself did not seem too
dirty, so Jeanne sat down on it carefully, holding onto the
side of the wagon for support as the wagon jounced along.
When she was settled, she looked around at her companions. It was difficult to tell too much about them in the
darkness, but the six cowboys all seemed to be cut from
the same cloth. They were young, dressed in rough range
clothes and floppy hats, and they were very drunk.

One of them leaned forward, bringing himself close
enough for her to smell the whiskey on his breath, and
peered intently at her. Jeanne tried to ignore him, but
after a moment, he said, "You're a saloon gal, ain't you?"

"I'm a blackjack dealer," Jeanne told him, trying to
avoid giving more information.

"I seen you someplace not long ago," the cowboy
went on. "Let's see . . . the Black Bull—yeah, that's it!"

He extended his hand with the exaggerated care of a man who has had too much to drink and knows it. "My name is Clovis Fancher, ma'am."

Jeanne was not sure whether she should shake his hand or not. So far the men had been polite enough, but when they got out of town, they might decide to have a little fun with this saloon girl they were helping. She did not want to do anything to encourage them.

She was spared the decision. Clovis Fancher gave a sudden moan and lunged for the side of the wagon, hanging his head over and suffering the same torments inflicted on Jeanne behind the undertaker's the night before. He was right next to Jeanne, and she found herself resting a hand on his back to steady him. The cowboy called Gil positioned himself on the other side of Clovis and helped out, as well.

"Hope you don't take offense, ma'am," Gil said during a momentary lull when Clovis was quiet. "Clovis don't mean no harm; he just don't know when to put the cork back in the bottle!"

Jeanne shook her head tiredly. "No offense," she assured Gil.

"We didn't get into town until midafternoon, and since we was leaving just after sundown, Clovis figured he had to pack a full day's drinkin' into four or five hours."

Up on the driver's seat, Luther shook his head in disgust. "Young fools don't never learn," he said to no one in particular. "They always think they're the first ones to ever buck the tiger."

The lights of Albuquerque were fading into the night behind the wagon. Jeanne still listened anxiously for the pounding of hoofbeats that would signal pursuit by Landreth's men, but they did not come. Everything appeared to be quiet. Using the cover of darkness to conceal what she was doing, she reached into the bosom of her dress and withdrew the papers she had taken from Landreth's desk. She had seen a lantern hanging on the driver's seat when she climbed onto the wagon, and now she asked Luther if he would mind lighting it.

"Hand it back here, Luther," Gil put in. "I'll light it for the lady."

"All right. Here," Luther said as he picked up the lantern and gave it to Gil. "Mind you don't set the wagon on fire, though."

"I won't." Gil set the lantern on the planks between him and Jeanne and scratched a match into life. "You worry too much, Luther."

"Somebody's got to," the driver muttered.

Gil lowered the chimney when the wick was lit, and the lantern cast a soft glow over the wagon bed. Aware that she was being watched by all the cowboys except Clovis Fancher, who was snoring softly now, Jeanne leaned closer to the light and started scanning the words on the papers. The first few documents were innocuous enough, simple correspondence about the business details of running the Black Bull.

Jeanne's mind began to drift back over what she already knew about Darryl Landreth. For starters, that was not his real name. Jeanne was not sure by what name he had been christened, but in the years since he had used many different ones. Landreth was only the latest in a long series. And he had even more crimes in his background than he did names. Forger, swindler, counterfeiter, common thief . . . and murderer. That was Darryl Landreth. He had killed at least one man, probably more. Jeanne knew for certain that he had murdered one of the victims of a confidence scheme when the man discovered the swindle and confronted him. It was that man's family who had hired the Pinkerton Detective Agency in this case. Though he had beaten the murder charge, they hoped the agency could find enough evidence of other crimes to jail Landreth for most of his remaining life. A suspect in many crimes, he had so far been successful in eluding justice.

That was going to change, if she had anything to do with it. Darryl Landreth was going to pay for his crimes.

Jeanne's concentration had been wandering, she realized with a sudden start as the words she had been idly scanning jerked her attention back to the paper. Her eyes narrowed as she frowned at the page. Then, as the full weight of what she was reading sank in, she felt her heart begin to pound.

She riffled through the rest of the sheets. They were all letters to Landreth, most of them short notes that bore the same signature at the bottom. Jeanne recognized the name. The man who had written the letters had been, until the year before, an important official in the territorial government in Santa Fe. When General Lew Wallace had become governor, however, this particular official, along with others of the so-called Santa Fe Ring, had been driven out of office, bringing to an end a notorious era of graft and corruption. And now, a year later, the man was involved with Darryl Landreth.

Though the notes were couched in cautious language, the hints were there between the lines. Landreth and the former official were planning some scheme that was nearing its culmination. And given the backgrounds of the two men, Jeanne was willing to bet that their plan was illegal. Just how sinister it was would be hard to say from the evidence she had now, but these letters were sufficient proof that something ominous was going to happen—which meant that they were more than simply incriminating to Landreth. They could tie him in with something explosive, something that perhaps would reach into the halls of the territorial capitol itself.

Landreth had to know by now that she had taken the letters. He would be coming after her with a vengeance. As long as she had them, she was fleeing for her very life.

"Ma'am, you look mighty worried about something," Gil said from beside her, startling her. "What's the matter? Bad news in them letters?"

"Unexpected news," Jeanne replied after a moment. She swayed slightly as the wagon rocked and bounced over the rough trail. Right now she could not worry too much about the implications of the letters. If she was going to stay alive, she had to take this one step at a time.

"Anything I can help you with?" Gil asked as she folded the papers into a compact sheaf and slipped them all into one of the envelopes.

Jeanne smiled slightly and shook her head. "I'm afraid I'll have to handle this by myself. By the way, where are all of you headed? I never did ask."

"We're on our way back to the Rockin' K, about

twenty miles north of Albuquerque. That's the brand we ride for." Gil chuckled. "It'll be close to dawn when we get there—and I reckon we'll all catch hell from the foreman for comin' in hung over, too."

"Damn right you will," Luther put in from the driver's seat.

Jeanne had heard of the Rocking K and knew its general location. "Does the stage line run through near here?" she asked.

Luther waved a hand toward the east. "The line runs over that way."

"Is there a station that wouldn't be too far out of your way?"

"There sure is," Gil told her. "The station at Slick Rock Creek is right close to where we're goin'. Ain't that right, Luther?"

"Reckon so," Luther grunted. "I don't mind takin' you there, miss, if that's where you want to go."

"Please," Jeanne said. "I'd really appreciate it."

"Our pleasure," Gil said with a big grin. He was the only one of the punchers still awake, Jeanne saw as she looked around the wagon. Evidently the liquor they had taken in had won out over their appreciation of a pretty woman.

She had been lucky so far, Jeanne thought. But luck might not last. It was fickle and could desert a person without a moment's notice. She had never been one to rely on luck, however. She relied on herself, and so far that had been enough.

But she had never been up against something like this before.

Chapter Three

Far to the north of Albuquerque, at a way station on the stage line between Santa Fe and Taos, a deputy U.S. marshal named Stuart Davis was staring up at the brilliant stars and grappling with his own private demons.

The young deputy marshal was leaning against a pine tree on the slope above the station, a pipe clenched between his teeth and a frown on his face. He was comfortable with the night, and the slight rustlings in the woods did not bother him. He was not afraid of anything around here. The Colt that rode in a well-oiled holster on his hip was enough to take care of any four-legged varmints.

Stuart's mind was somewhere else, remembering another day. . . .

Bright, brassy sunshine beating down, sweat dripping in his eyes and making them sting, the sudden boom of guns, the fiery tearing pain in his left arm, the sickening smell of blood . . .

It was all there, as vivid as the day it had happened. Stuart was beginning to think that the memories would always be there, lurking just behind him, ready to spring into view when he least expected them.

Stuart Davis looked older than his twenty-eight years. His lean face showed the lines and creases of a life spent outdoors in all kinds of weather. His dark, curly hair was touched with gray here and there, as was the short, neat beard that he wore.

He reached up and took the pipe out of his mouth. It was cold, and he did not remember when it had gone out.

Down below in the corral next to the station, Stuart's father, George Davis, was checking on the horses, settling them down for the night. Stuart could see him moving around in the corral and could hear his irascible voice as he talked to the animals. It was nice to think that some things stayed the same, and George Davis had not altered his routines in years—all the years that Stuart could remember, in fact. Stuart had been born here at this way station, his mother giving him life while giving up her own in the middle of a winter storm that had covered the hills with several feet of snow. George did not talk much about that night, and Stuart respected his father's wishes and had never pressured him for the details.

He started walking slowly down the hill toward the station. Even though it was summer, the nights around here were chilly, and he was grateful for the lightweight jacket he was wearing. He knocked the ashes out of his pipe and slipped it into a pocket as he walked, his boots crunching on twigs and loose gravel.

Stuart raised his right hand and rubbed his left upper arm. The wound there had healed, but it still ached at times, and his left arm had never regained its full strength. He could live with that, he supposed, and it was beginning to look as if he would have to.

He reached the station building and opened the rough wooden door. Inside, the place was all one windowless room, with only the one door to defend, though there were rifle slits cut here and there in the walls. There had never been much Indian trouble in this area, but bandits had raised hell from time to time. It was best to have a place that could be defended easily.

The station building was comfortably warm, heated by the wood cook stove on which simmered a pot of beans for the next day's passengers. A candle was burning on the big table in the center of the room. Stuart walked past it to a cabinet, where he found a bottle of whiskey and a glass. He took the bottle and the glass back to the table, pulled a chair around with his foot, and straddled it. He pulled the cork on the bottle and poured a drink, not spilling a drop of the amber liquid. A slight smile pulled at his lips. At least he still had a steady hand for some things.

He did not drink the whiskey right away but instead left it sitting on the table. Crossing his arms on the back of the chair, he regarded the glass thoughtfully. He had never been much of a drinking man until the last few months, and he was not sure why it held such a fascination for him now. His slender, strong fingers reached out for the glass.

Until three months earlier, Stuart had been working out of Denver. Officially, he was now on leave from the marshal's office, recuperating from injuries suffered in the line of duty. Unofficially, he was growing more sure all the time that his days as a peace officer were over. It took an almost reckless confidence to stand behind a badge against overwhelming odds; he was afraid that he might have lost the keen edge necessary to be a top-notch lawman.

He lifted the glass to his mouth.

The door opened and George Davis came in, moving with a spryness that belied his rheumatism. He sucked on his two remaining teeth as his son downed the whiskey. Then he said, "That won't help Corey none, boy."

"I know that," Stuart said, carefully putting the empty glass on the table. He thought about his fellow deputy marshal, who now was dead. "Nothing's going to help Corey now, is it?"

"Don't reckon it'd do any good to tell you for the hundredth time that it weren't your fault, son."

Stuart shook his head. "Nope."

George sighed and went to the stove to give the pot of beans a stir. Stuart knew in his head that his father was right. But his stomach told a different story, the story of a failed mission. . . .

It was a hot day, even though summer was still a couple of months away. Stuart Davis and Corey Moss, occupying the rear seat in the stagecoach, braced themselves against the rocking motion of the coach and waited tensely, Stuart watching to the right, Corey to the left. There were Winchesters resting across their laps, and their hands never strayed far from the butts of their Colts.

The outlaws who had been holding up the Denver

coach on a fairly regular basis were due for a big surprise on this run.

The driver and the shotgun guard were the usual ones for this trip, but the two deputy marshals were the only passengers. The company had let it leak that the coach was transporting a sizable amount of cash. That was a lie, of course, designed to lure the bandits out of their hiding place. Their routine was simple and always the same. A felled log blocked the road just around one of the many blind curves along the route, and when the stage was forced to an abrupt stop, the bandits would come out of their hiding places in the brush, their guns drawn on the driver and guard.

Today was going to be a different story, however. Stuart and Corey, both tough, experienced deputies, would see to that.

Stuart lifted his hat, a black Stetson with silver disks decorating the band, and used a sleeve to mop sweat off his forehead. "Hot for this time of year," he said idly.

"That's the truth," Corey replied. He and Stuart had worked together many times in the past, and there was an ease between the two men that made for a good team.

"They should be making their move pretty soon," Stuart said, his keen eyes taking in every detail of the landscape the coach was passing.

"If they're going to. Could be they decided to pass on this one."

Stuart laughed shortly. "Not likely. They're a greedy bunch, and they must know this coach is supposed to be carrying a lot of loot."

"We'll see, I reckon." Corey put a hand against the side of the coach to steady himself as it swayed around a hairpin turn.

Suddenly the driver let out a startled yell and grabbed the brake lever, pulling back on it with all his strength while hauling in on the reins with his other hand. Inside the stage, Stuart and Corey were both thrown forward by the abrupt stop. They snatched up their Winchesters, levering shells into the chambers, and kicked open both doors, ready to dive out and start blazing away.

"What in tarnation?" the guard on the box exclaimed.

There were no gunshots. Stuart knew that if this was a holdup, the outlaws should have been charging out of the brush by now.

The driver leaned over and said to his passengers, "You boys might as well come out and take a look at this. I never seen anything like it."

Stuart dropped through one door, Corey the other, and they walked up beside the box. The four men stared at the spectacle blocking the trail up ahead. There was the usual fallen log, and propped against it was a crude dummy, more like a scarecrow. The dummy had a shotgun cradled in its arms, and a bandanna was tied across its blank face like a mask.

A piece of paper was pinned to the dummy's chest, and Stuart could see writing on it. His eyes narrowed; this could still be a trap. "You boys get ready for trouble," he said. "I'm going to see what that paper says."

He moved forward quickly, reaching out to rip the message off the dummy. He scanned the scrawled writing: *Yore cumpany is a pack of lyars Thers no gold on thet stage You wont ly agin you basterds*

The ruse had not worked; the bandits had not been fooled by the story that the stage line had circulated, and the dummy and the message were their way of gloating. The last line of the message, unless Stuart missed his guess, was a threat.

He jerked his head around and yelled to Corey, "It's a trap! Get in the stage!" Even as he shouted, he was dropping the message and breaking into a run.

Corey hesitated a second, startled by the sudden turn of events, then started to spin around and reach for the door of the coach. Stuart saw him stagger and simultaneously heard the boom of a rifle. There was another blast from the trees near the road, and Corey bent double as though he had been punched in the belly. Once more he reached for the door. His grasping fingers missed, and he crumpled in the dust of the trail.

"Corey!"

Stuart ran toward his friend, seeing out of the corner of his eye the blossoms of flame from the guns of the hidden outlaws. The driver and the guard were returning the fire, and the shots blended together and rolled through the hills like thunder.

Corey looked up, his arms crossed against his midsection as he tried to hold himself together. His eyes met Stuart's for an instant before the life went out of them, leaving them as hard and glassy as marbles.

Stuart fell to his knees beside his fellow deputy and called his name one last time, but he knew it was too late. He heard bullets slamming into the coach just over his head, and the sound of death so close made him force everything else out of his mind. He threw the Winchester to his shoulder and began to fire toward the ambushers, working the lever so fast that the action became a blur.

A slug caught him in the arm and threw him back against the wheel of the coach. His whole left arm and shoulder suddenly went numb. When he glanced down, he could see the bright flow of blood staining his sleeve, but he could not feel the pain yet. He dropped the rifle, unable to use it one-handed, and jerked out his Colt, triggering it toward the trees as fast as he could.

The shotgun guard was no longer firing; he had been hit in the head. The driver continued to shoot with one hand while trying to control the terrified team with the other. One of the outlaws' bullets caught him in the chest, making him drop his gun and the reins and fall heavily off the box. The horses bolted then, and as the wheel jerked away from Stuart, the hub clipped him on the side of the head. He sprawled in the trail, the Colt slipping from his suddenly nerveless fingers.

He was not aware of it then, but the team dragged the coach toward the barricade and then swerved wildly and tried to go down the slope to the side. The coach turned over, rolling down the hill, unfortunately taking the horses with it.

By the time Stuart woke up in a pool of his own blood, he was the only one left alive. The driver, the guard, Corey . . . all were dead. Even the horses had been killed by the wreck.

It was a long walk to the next way station. The doctor who treated him later said that the effort should have killed him, considering the loss of blood he had suffered despite the crude tourniquet he had fashioned. But Stuart had made that walk, had reported the ambush and the death of his companions.

And anger for those deaths had walked with him . . . every step of the way. . . .

Three months later, the anger and the memories were still his constant companions, despite the consoling knowledge that the gang had been wiped out in a gun battle a few weeks after. The only time he came close to forgetting was when he had been drinking.

Stuart reached out and replaced the cork in the bottle. His father, watching over his shoulder from the stove, sighed in relief and turned back to tending his beans. George was a good hand with horses and he could keep this station running the way it was supposed to, but dealing with Stuart's lost confidence was just more than he knew how to handle.

Stuart suddenly lifted his head. "Somebody's coming," he announced.

"Couldn't be. Tonight's stage left hours ago," George said.

"I don't care. I hear horses, several of them."

"I don't hear nothin', but you know I don't hear so good no more, boy. Wonder who in tarnation it could be?"

"I reckon we'll find out," Stuart replied, a slight smile tugging at the corners of his mouth. His father had been complaining about his hearing for years, yet Stuart had noticed that George seemed to hear most things that he *wanted* to hear.

Stuart stood and put the bottle of whiskey back in the cabinet. He paused a moment, rubbed a hand over his face, and then headed for the door.

On the slope above the station, near the spot where Stuart had been standing earlier, four men reined in their horses and looked down at the building and the corral in the clearing below. They had been riding for a long time, having left Taos early that morning after receiving a telegram from Albuquerque.

As they paused, one of the men spat on the ground

and said, "Ain't likely this Fontanne woman would've got this far so soon, Chuck. Landreth said she just left Albuquerque last night."

"I know it," the one called Chuck growled. "But Landreth's wire said for us to head south and check all the stage stations on the way. He's probably sendin' Briggs north from Albuquerque to do the same thing, and we'll meet up in Santa Fe."

"Hell, it don't matter to me," one of the other men put in. "Long as I'm gettin' paid, I'll run whatever errands Landreth wants run."

"Damn right," the fourth man agreed.

"Let's head on down there then," Chuck said. "You boys let me do the talkin'. Landreth wants this done quiet-like."

He heeled his horse into motion and led the other three men down the hill to the way station.

Stuart eased the door of the station open and stood slightly to the side, not wanting to present too much of a silhouetted target as he peered out into the night. The station was far enough out in the country that it paid to be careful how you opened a door at night. His years as a peace officer only reinforced those cautious instincts.

"Four men," he told George a moment later, his keen eyes picking out the moving shapes in the shadows. "They don't seem to be in a hurry."

George came to Stuart's side and looked out past him. "Lookin' for a meal, more'n likely."

The men rode into the clearing and reined up in front of the station. The one in the lead leaned on the pommel of his saddle and nodded to Stuart and George. "Evenin'," he said.

"Howdy," George replied. "Something we can do for you gents?"

"Been ridin' for quite a spell. Any chance of gettin' some grub and a drink of whiskey around here?"

George cast a quick glance at Stuart. "We've got whiskey," he said flatly. "There's some stew left over from dinner, and I reckon I could rustle up some cornbread to go with it. How's that suit you, mister?"

"Sounds fine." The man started to swing down off his horse, his companions following suit.

"Four bits apiece," George added. "I'm as hospitable a man as you'll find in these parts, but the stage company don't pay me for feedin' nobody. Even the coach passengers got to pay."

"Fair enough." The man nodded.

Stuart moved over to the stove and studied the four men out of the corner of his eye as they trooped into the building and hung their hats on the pegs driven into the wall just beside the doorway. They were all cut from the same cloth: burly men in worn, rough clothing, all four of them packing side irons.

One of them nodded to Stuart as they sat down at the table and said, "Howdy, amigo."

"Howdy," Stuart replied quietly.

It was not uncommon for travelers to stop at the station for a meal. All kinds of people used the road, from lone men on horseback to whole families of settlers in wagons. But these men made Stuart uneasy. He tried not to stare too intently, but there was something familiar about a couple of them, including the one who had spoken to him. He had seen them somewhere before—or he had seen their pictures. Perhaps on a wanted poster?

That thought was all the connection that Stuart needed to make the leap of recognition. He *had* seen the pictures of two of them on wanted posters. They were outlaws, and Stuart knew that if he thought about it long enough, he would probably be able to remember their names. The question now was what was he going to do about it?

Even though he was on leave of absence, he was still a deputy marshal. It was his duty to arrest wanted outlaws, whenever and wherever he encountered them. And there was a good chance that the other two men were wanted, as well. If he let them go, they would almost certainly go on to commit more crimes. People would die at their hands; Stuart was sure of that.

But the quarters were close here in the way station. If he started any gunplay, George might be hit by a stray shot. He would wind up dead . . . like Corey Moss.

Stuart's eyes were downcast, studying the hard-packed

earthen floor, as he struggled with the decision that could mean life or death for all of them.

George took the whiskey bottle from the cabinet and brought it to the table. "I'll get you some glasses," he said.

The leader of the four men held up the bottle and considered the level of the liquor inside. It was about three-fourths full. "Don't bother with the glasses," he said, digging out a coin and spinning it onto the table. "We'll take what's left, if that's all right."

"All right with me," George said, glancing once again at Stuart, who seemed to be paying no attention to the exchange.

The man took the cork from the bottle and tilted it to his lips, his throat working as he swallowed thirstily. From his reaction and the looks on the faces of the other men, their trail had indeed been a long and dusty one. When the man was through with the bottle, he passed it on to one of the others.

"Where are you boys headed?" George asked as he measured out the ingredients for the bread.

"South, no particular place," the leader said, watching with avid eyes as the bottle was passed around the table. "We're lookin' for somebody," he added. "Maybe one of you saw her."

"I see dang near everybody who comes through this neck of the woods," George replied. "Who's this gal you're lookin' for?"

"She's a redheaded girl, real pretty." The man nodded at one of his companions. "She's Ben's sister, and we're tryin' to get the two of 'em together. She was probably headin' north."

George shook his head. "I don't recollect any redheaded gals goin' through on the stage in either direction. How about you, Stuart?"

Stuart looked up and saw the sudden interest with which the men regarded him. From their expressions, it was clear that they were very interested in finding that redheaded woman, though he did not for a moment believe the story about her being the sister of one of them. It was more likely she was a woman the man was sweet on.

"I haven't seen anyone who looks like that," he said

shortly. His eyes met those of the man who had spoken to him earlier. The man was frowning at him now, and Stuart could almost see the wheels of his brain turning. With a sinking feeling, he realized that the man had seen him before and was trying to place him. If the man remembered that Stuart was a deputy marshal, there was going to be trouble.

The man was peering intently at him in the lantern light. His frown deepened, and he asked, "Don't I know you from somewhere, friend?"

"I don't think so," Stuart said. "You must be thinking of somebody else."

"Naw, I'd swear it was you." The man lifted a hand to rub his jaw in thought, and then his eyes suddenly widened in realization. "It was in Denver!" he exclaimed. "You was comin' out of the marshal's office—"

The leader of the men looked sharply at his companion and snapped, "What are you jabberin' about, Jud?"

Jud's hand left his stubbled jaw and flashed downward. "He's a lawman!" he howled, coming up out of his chair. He clawed his pistol out of its holster.

Stuart knew he had no choice. He went for his gun, letting his instincts take over. The Colt cleared leather smoothly, a second behind the other man's. Jud's gun blasted first, but Stuart's was so close behind it that the double roar sounded like one. Stuart felt the bullet slap through the air beside his ear at the same instant that Jud rocked backward. His free hand clutched at his chest, and the gun in his other hand exploded again, this time sending the slug into the heavy wooden table.

Jud slid to the side, falling heavily, the front of his shirt splattered bright red.

The other three men surged to their feet, grabbing for their own guns. Stuart whirled toward them, vaguely aware of a flicker of motion behind them.

"Have some beans, boys!" George Davis yelled, dumping the simmering contents of the big iron pot over the head of one man. He slammed it sideways then, into the head of another man.

Stuart was facing the leader of the four strangers. The man's pistol was out now and coming up fast. Stuart triggered twice, the reports deafening in the close quarters. Both bullets smacked into the man's chest, and he went down with his gun unfired.

The one who had had hot water and beans dumped on his head was howling in pain and grabbing blindly for his pistol. Stuart lunged forward and lashed out with his Colt, and the barrel thudded against the man's head. He sprawled forward across the table with a low moan and then lay still.

Stuart took a deep breath and listened to the blood pound in his head as his pulse raced. The fourth man was down, too, a victim of the heavy iron pot that George now put back on the stove. He was out cold, just like the one that Stuart had clouted.

George looked down at the mess on the floor and shook his shaggy head. "Waste of a lot o' beans," he clucked in dismay. "I was wonderin' when you'd make your play, son."

"I thought you moved awfully quick," Stuart said. "You knew there was going to be trouble, didn't you?"

"Hell, I knowed them boys was on the dodge just by lookin' at 'em. Figgered it was just a matter of time until you took 'em."

Stuart went over to a storage bin in the corner of the room and took out several pieces of harness rigging that George kept there for repair jobs that were sometimes needed on the passing coaches. He knelt beside the unconscious outlaws and quickly lashed their hands behind them, yanking a little harder on the knots than he had to.

The two men he had shot were dead. He had known that without even checking, though he should have confirmed it before attending to the two who were unconscious. It was funny how the things that were trained into a man started to slip away, he thought. At least he had taken care of this situation with no harm coming to his father. But that did not mean he was competent to go back to being a deputy; a lot of this had been luck.

"I'll take those two and the bodies into Santa Fe and turn them over to Sheriff Crider." Stuart's smile was grim as he went on, "Maybe the live ones won't mind spending a few more hours with their friends."

Stuart and George hauled the four outlaws outside. It was an unpleasant task to tie them onto their saddles, but it did not take long.

"You sure you want to start into town with them tonight?" George asked.

"I know the trail to Santa Fe," Stuart told him. "I don't want them around the station."

"Reckon I can understand that. The dead 'uns are apt to get a mite fragrant 'fore mornin'."

Stuart nodded. What his father said was true enough, but that was not the real reason he wanted to take the men on into Santa Fe. They were a reminder of trouble, and he wanted them off his hands as soon as possible.

Back in the station building, George started cleaning up the mess the beans had made. He glanced up at Stuart and said, "You handled 'em good, son. Real good. Just like always."

"No," Stuart said, his eyes faraway. He was seeing something else again. "Not like always."

Chapter Four

J eanne Townsend finally dozed a bit in the wagon, swaying as the vehicle rolled over the rough trails. When she awoke after a particularly sharp jolt, her neck was stiff and sore. She spent a minute rubbing it and working the muscles to loosen them and then looked around to get her bearings.

The sky was gray in the east, and the trees surrounding the trail were visible now. In the distance on both sides, dark mountains thrust up into the lightening sky. The stars faded as Jeanne watched, and the sun suddenly seemed to leap over the eastern horizon, spreading yellow light over the rugged territory.

"Purty, ain't it?" Gil said quietly from beside her.

She glanced over at him. She had thought that he was asleep, since he was leaning back with his hat tipped forward over his eyes, but she saw now that he had raised his head slightly.

"Yes, it is," she replied. "I haven't had many chances lately to see the sun rise over the mountains."

"Reckon not, workin' in a saloon like you been doin'. Ever thought about givin' it up? You seem like too much of a lady for a life like that."

Jeanne smiled. "I've thought about it," she said.

Gil would be surprised if he knew she was not really a saloon girl, almost as surprised as he would be if he found out she actually was a Pinkerton agent.

As she glanced around the wagon bed, she saw that the other cowboys were still asleep, though a few of them were beginning to stir. Up front on the driver's seat, Luther was yawning and trying to stay awake as he kept the team on the trail. He looked over his shoulder and said, "We ought to be gettin' to that way station soon, ma'am. Should be just over the next couple of rises."

"I appreciate you taking me there," Jeanne told him. "I know you must be tired and want to get to your ranch."

Luther grinned and jerked a thumb in Gil's direction. "It's this boy here and them other yahoos who're goin' to pay for last night," he said. "I ain't hung over, and I ain't got to get out and ride the range today like them. No, ma'am, I'm headin' for the bunkhouse and a few hours sleep."

"Not until you fix us some breakfast, you ol' lunkhead," Gil said.

Luther laughed shortly. "Fend for yourself, boy."

Jeanne lowered her head and smiled as she listened to the good-natured wrangling between the two men. Their life was hard but simple, without all the worries that she had. On the other hand, they had to cope with the tedium of ranch life. She did not have that problem. Her life was dangerous enough at times, but it was hardly ever boring.

Yet a part of her wished she could put her responsibilities away for a while and travel on to the ranch with these cowboys. She would have enjoyed spending more time with them. But hiding out with them would only bring Darryl Landreth and his vengeance down on their heads. Jeanne did not want that. She wanted to stay on her own as much as possible, so that innocent people would not be endangered.

"There's the station down yonder," Luther said as he hauled back on the lines and brought the team to a halt.

Jeanne turned around and got up on her knees so that she could see. The wagon was stopped on the top of a ridge, and down below in a little valley was the way station. It was a low, square adobe building with a corral out back. She could see a man, probably the stationmaster, moving around the corral as he tended to the small herd of horses kept there.

Off to the right, the fairly broad, well-traveled stage

road led into the valley from the south. From the ridge where the wagon sat, however, only a narrow rutted trail led down the steep hill into the valley. Jeanne studied it for a moment and then said, "I can walk down from here. You don't have to take the wagon down that trail, Luther."

He spat off to the side. "Don't mind. This team can handle it, and so can I."

"I know that. But it's not necessary." Jeanne smiled ruefully. "Besides, the walk will do me good, get out some of the kinks."

The other cowboys woke up now, roused by the fact that the wagon had come to a stop. Their pained expressions were ample evidence of the way their heads felt, yet all of them summoned a smile when Jeanne said good-bye to them.

Gil hopped out of the wagon, wincing as his booted feet hit the ground and jarred him. Then he held up a hand to help Jeanne down. He took her other hand as she climbed over the wheel and stepped to the ground, and then he said with a grin, "What would you do, ma'am, if I was to steal me a kiss?"

"Gil . . ." Luther said in a tone of warning.

"I would remember you a bit less kindly," Jeanne told the cowboy, trying to make her voice stern.

Gil nodded regretfully and then a look of determination came over his face. "Ah, hell," he said, pulling her close and tipping her head so that his lips could come down on hers. Jeanne did not resist. The kiss was a short one, and Gil's grin was wider as he pulled away. "It was worth it," he declared.

Jeanne could not bring herself to do anything but smile back at him.

"Get in the wagon, boy," Luther said. "We got to get to the ranch, and this lady wants to get on about her business without some fresh cowboy holdin' her up."

Jeanne turned toward him. "Thank you again for the ride. You saved my life." That was no exaggeration, she knew, though Luther took it for one.

He reached up and tugged on the brim of his hat. "Glad we could be of service, ma'am." He glanced back to see that Gil had returned to the wagon bed, and then he flapped the lines and called out to the team. The wagon rolled away, its occupants waving at Jeanne.

She returned the waves and the smiles and then turned and started down the trail toward the way station.

Micah Donahue had been handling horses for a lot of years, and he knew when they sensed something. He tossed down the bale of hay he had just carried into the corral and turned to study the ridge to the west of the station. The horses acted as if something up there was bothering them.

It was a beautiful morning. Micah had been getting up at dawn for as long as he could remember, but he still enjoyed it, especially on days like this when the air was clean and fresh and the sun was bright and warm, burning off the shreds of mist that were still floating below the trees.

Suddenly, Micah's eyes widened. He stared at the trail leading down from the ridge, unable for a moment to believe what he was seeing.

There was a woman coming down that trail, a beautiful redheaded woman in a scandalous gown of green silk. . . .

"Micah!" The sharp tones of his wife, Alice, came from the back door of the station building. "Who in the Lord's name is that?"

Micah shook his head. "I'm afraid I don't know, sweetheart," he said. "But she sure is . . . unusual looking."

As she approached the station, Jeanne saw the way the man and the woman were looking at her. She had expected to surprise whoever was there, and it appeared that she was succeeding. She smiled at the older couple as she drew near and raised a hand in greeting. "Hello! Is this the way station?"

Micah nodded. "Surely is. I'm Micah Donahue, the stationmaster." As his wife cleared her throat, he hurried on, "And this is my missus, Alice."

Jeanne came to a stop a few feet away and smiled wearily. "I'm glad to meet you," she said sincerely. "My name is Jeanne Townsend." She was glad to be able to drop the pseudonym and get back to her real name, and she knew it was the wisest thing to do, since Landreth knew her only by the name Jeanne Fontanne.

Micah, a tall, grizzled old-timer, rubbed his beard-stubbled jaw and said slowly, "Pardon me for asking, ma'am, but what the devil are you doing out here on foot?"

"I want to catch the next stage going north," Jeanne replied, not really answering his question. "There will be one today, won't there?"

Micah nodded. "Yes, ma'am, about noon. Where you headed?"

"Denver." Jeanne glanced over at Alice Donahue and saw a spare, tight-featured woman of middle years who was regarding her suspiciously. Jeanne went on, "Would it be possible to get something to eat? I can pay."

"I was just fixing breakfast," Alice said, her tone wary. "Come on inside." She glanced at her husband and went on sharply, "You best get back to your chores, Micah."

He nodded. "Yeah," he mumbled, looking down at the ground. "Reckon I better."

Jeanne followed Alice Donahue into the station, feeling none too welcome. She had seen the way Micah was looking at her—as if he had not seen anything nearly as good-looking in a long time—and she supposed she could not blame his wife for her reaction. At the moment, however, she was not concerned about any domestic friction she might cause. The smell of bacon and eggs and fresh bread was painfully reminding her that she had not eaten in more than a day.

Alice gestured at a long, rough-hewn table. "Sit down," she said. "I'll get you a cup of coffee."

"I can get it," Jeanne said, spotting the coffeepot on the wood-burning stove. "I'll help you with the meal, too."

Alice's back stiffened even more. "I can handle it, thank you. You just have a seat." It was more an order than a request.

Jeanne sighed and sat down. She had offended the older woman by offering to help. No doubt Alice felt that Jeanne was trying to encroach on her territory. Jeanne regretted the misunderstanding, but it was not surprising;

she had never spent enough time in a kitchen or around other women to know exactly what protocol to follow.

Alice brought over a steaming cup of coffee. "Food'll be ready in a few minutes."

"Thank you." Jeanne sipped the hot liquid, grateful for its bracing effect, and sat quietly for the next several minutes.

Alice brought three platters of food to the table, balancing them precariously, as Micah came in from outside. He sat down at the head of the table while his wife placed one of the platters in front of their guest. Jeanne's hunger had grown even more demanding in the time she had been here, and she was ready to dig in. But as Alice sat down, she and Micah clasped their hands, and Micah muttered a brief prayer. Jeanne waited politely until he was finished.

For a few minutes after that, the three of them were silent as they ate. The food tasted delicious, but Jeanne did not know how much of that was indeed the food and how much was her ravenous hunger. Then Alice said, "You never told us what you're doing out here."

Jeanne took a deep breath. She had been thinking about that very subject, knowing that Alice probably would not be satisfied until she had answered.

"I came from Albuquerque," she said. "I was working in a saloon there."

"Reckon we could tell that," Micah said cheerfully. He looked at his food as Alice shot a barbed glance at him.

"How'd you get way out here?"

"I caught a ride last night with a wagonload of cowboys," Jeanne answered truthfully. "They were on their way to the Rocking K."

Micah nodded. "I know some of them boys. They're not a bad bunch."

"There were very kind to me. I . . . I don't know what I would have done if they hadn't come along and helped me get away."

Alice frowned. "Get away from what?"

"Not what. Who. There was a man . . . the man I work for at the saloon . . ." Jeanne put her fork down and struggled with the words. "He tried to . . . to force himself on me. I wish I'd never gone to work there!"

Alice's expression had softened somewhat as Jeanne spoke, but she was not ready to dismiss her suspicions. "Then why did you go to work in a place like a saloon?" she asked.

"To get money," Jeanne said. "I was trying to save up some money so that Tommy Lee and I could get married. . . ." A single tear rolled down her cheek.

Jeanne let the fabricated story all come out then—the story of how all she wanted to do was marry a young man named Tommy Lee and settle down on his farm and raise a bunch of kids. Unfortunately they could not get married until Tommy Lee was able to pay back some money he owed, so that he would not lose the farm his father had settled.

Though most of it was a lie, there really had been a boy named Tommy Lee, and at one time she had thought about marrying him. That had been a long time ago—a very long time ago, when she was a young girl living in Chicago.

Jeanne felt guilty for spinning such an outrageous yarn and doing it so convincingly that the Donahues believed it completely. Like the cowboys from the Rocking K, they accepted the melodramatic story, though Jeanne had embellished it quite a bit more for Micah and Alice. As she spoke, they became more and more sympathetic, Alice losing all the hardness in her face and Micah looking at her more like a daughter.

"What an ordeal!" Alice exclaimed when Jeanne finished telling about the all-night ride in the wagon. "You must be exhausted."

"I slept a little in the wagon." Jeanne smiled slightly. "It wasn't very restful, though."

"I should say not, riding in a horrible old wagon with a bunch of roughneck cowboys," Micah put in.

"They were all perfect gentlemen."

Micah snorted. "If that bunch was perfect at anything, it was the first time in their lives. You need some real rest, young lady, in a bed."

Alice stood up. "That's what I was thinking. The

northbound stage won't be here until noon, at least. You can get several hours sleep between now and then."

"I don't want to put you out . . ." Jeanne began.

"Nonsense! You won't be putting us out. Will she, Micah?"

"Not at all," Micah confirmed. "Alice, you go fix up our bed for her."

"That's just what I was going to do. Get the girl something more to eat, why don't you?"

"No, really, I have plenty as it is, and I don't want you going to any more trouble," Jeanne protested, honestly embarrassed now by the way these people had reacted so generously to her lies.

"It's no trouble," Micah said gruffly.

Alice hesitated and then said, "We've got a daughter about your age. Back in St. Louis, she is. Sometimes we get to missing her something fierce. So let us do this for you, Jeanne. For her sake."

Jeanne nodded, unable to refuse such a request.

She finished her meal, and then Alice led her into the small bedroom. Actually, it was just a curtained-off area of the big main room, but there was a bed there, a fourposter that Micah had obviously spent many hours carving.

"We'll get you up in plenty of time to catch the stage," Alice assured her. "You just rest and don't worry about a thing. I'm sure everything will turn out all right for you and Tommy Lee."

"Thank you," Jeanne said. She sank down on the bed and sighed in spite of herself. The mattress was a little lumpy, but it felt like heaven right at the moment.

Alice smiled and pulled closed the curtain.

Jeanne stretched out and closed her eyes. The papers concealed in the bosom of her dress gave a faint crinkle, and she thought about taking them out and looking them over again. But her eyes did not want to open; it felt so good just to rest.

Now if only Landreth and his men did not show up before the stage came through, maybe she would have a chance to get away for good, to the safety of the agency in Denver. She certainly did not want anything bad to happen to Micah and Alice. They had treated her well, better than she deserved after the story she had handed them. . . .

Without really being aware of it, she drifted off to sleep.

Jeanne stretched, feeling the sheets beneath her. It was good to be in a bed again, a real bed instead of the cot she had used in the little room at the Black Bull. She kept her eyes closed for a moment, unwilling to wake up completely. If she did, she knew she would have to return to the dangerous shadow world she had inhabited for so long, a world where being on the run was not that uncommon. She knew, however, that hiding behind a sleepy veil was not going to help. Eventually she would have to get up, and then she would have to deal with the fact that Darryl Landreth had undoubtedly sent out men to find and kill her.

Jeanne sat up, the smile with which she had awakened gone now, her face set in grim lines. She swung her legs off the lumpy mattress and stood, stretching again for a moment to loosen her sleep-stiffened muscles. The curtain started to swing back, and Jeanne spun toward it, her instincts taking over. Her muscles tensed as she readied herself for trouble.

Alice Donahue stood there, looking slightly startled.

"Goodness," the older woman said. "I figured you'd still be asleep. I must have surprised you."

Jeanne willed herself to relax and summoned a smile. "I just woke up," she said. "What time is it?"

"Eleven-thirty. The stage will be here in half an hour or so. I thought you might like to freshen up, maybe eat some more, before it gets here."

"That sounds good." Jeanne nodded. She felt more than a little messy, after all she had been through.

"I've got a pot of water on the stove. You can use it to wash up," Alice said, as if reading her mind.

Jeanne followed Alice out into the big room, looking around to see where Micah was. Alice saw what she was doing and said, "Micah's out in the corral getting a fresh team ready to hitch up. I told him to give us a few minutes."

"Thank you," Jeanne replied as Alice brought the pan of water and a cloth over to the table.

Jeanne began slipping out of her clothes, carefully concealing the envelope of papers inside the folds of her dress. It felt good to get out of the tight, garish saloon dress. Standing in her sheer camisole and short petticoat, she took the cloth and washed herself, enjoying the feel of the warm water on her skin.

An idea occurred to her, and she said to Alice, "Do you think you might have an old dress you'd sell me?" She picked up the silken gown she had worn at the Black Bull and regarded it with a frown. "I'm tired of this thing. It's not something a decent woman should wear."

"That's the truth, honey. I'm sure I can find something that will fit you."

Alice went into the sleeping area and returned a moment later with a black woolen dress. The garment was very plain, Jeanne saw, but that did not bother her.

"You try this on," Alice told her.

Jeanne pulled the dress over her head, letting it settle into place and then fastening the long row of buttons that ran up the front of it. The buttons came all the way to her throat, which was quite a change from the revealing saloon dress.

"It might be kind of warm," Alice said apologetically. She gestured at her broad hips. "But it's the only thing I've still got that wouldn't be too big on you."

"It's fine," Jeanne assured her. The dress was going to be warm, all right, but the way it looked was more important. It was perfect for what she had in mind.

Jeanne pulled the pins from her hair, letting the rich red curls tumble loosely to her shoulders. Then she pulled them into a severe bun, pinning the new style firmly in place. That changed the shape of her face a bit, too, making it appear leaner and less sensuous. She had already scrubbed the gaudy makeup off her cheeks.

Alice was staring at her. "My lands, you don't look anything like you did!" she exclaimed. "I wouldn't have recognized you if I hadn't seen the change myself."

Jeanne smiled. "That's what I want. I want to put that part of my life behind me."

That was not quite the truth. She was not through with Darryl Landreth just yet. But changing her appearance would go a long way toward helping her accomplish her goals.

Alice was still shaking her head. "I'll get you some lunch," she said. "I just can't get over the change in you. You look like a schoolmarm now."

Before Jeanne could reply, there was a knock on the station door, and then it opened slowly. Micah stuck his head in and looked around. "You wake the lady up?" he asked his wife.

Alice jerked her head toward Jeanne. "There she is."

By then Micah had already spotted Jeanne standing beside the table, and his eyes widened as he looked at her and said, "Lordy mercy, what happened to you, ma'am?"

"Micah!" Alice scolded him for his bluntness.

"It's all right," Jeanne said. "I decided that the best way to put my past behind me was to make a change in the present, Mr. Donahue."

"Well, you made a change, all right," he said.

Jeanne sensed that he was slightly disappointed. He had preferred her more glamorous incarnation and had probably been looking forward to spending a little more time with her before she left on the next coach.

"Stage ought to be here soon," Micah went on. "Anything I can do for you before it gets here?"

Jeanne shook her head. "You've both been very kind to me. I don't know what I would have done if I hadn't been able to get here." She reached into the pocket of the saloon dress and took out her money. "I suppose I need to buy a ticket now, and I want to pay you for the meals and the dress."

"You don't owe me anything for the dress," Alice said from the stove. "It wasn't ever going to do me any more good. And the meals were on us."

"Oh, no, I don't mind paying," Jeanne began to protest.

"Reckon we got the right to be hospitable if we want," Micah said firmly. "As for your passage on the stage, well, that you can pay for. The company's got rules, you know."

Jeanne smiled, and when Micah told her the cost of a ticket, she peeled off a couple of bills from the roll of money. She handed them to Micah and then stowed the rest away in her bosom again, discreetly turning away while she did it. The money joined the papers she had taken from Landreth's office, already safely concealed while Alice had her back turned at the stove.

The meal was the same as what they had had for breakfast, but it was hot and filling, and Jeanne was grateful for it. Alice and Micah wanted to know what her plans were, and she told them that she intended to head for Denver, where she would rejoin Tommy Lee and they would go from there to his farm. After being married, of course, she added with an embarrassed smile. They would make it somehow, she insisted, despite the financial problems. Taking a job in a saloon just was not the answer.

As she listened to herself detailing the fantasy, she found herself wishing there was some truth to it. She knew deep down, however, that a life such as she was describing would end up boring her to tears if she really had to live it. She was used to more excitement.

As they were finishing their meal, the sound of a horn drifted in through the open door. Micah pushed his chair back and stood up. "There's the stage," he announced and went out to greet its arrival.

Alice hurried to the stove. "This is a meal stop," she explained. "We always eat before the passengers get here." She took down several heavy plates from a cabinet and started filling them with food.

Jeanne had finished her food, so she stood and asked, "Is there anything I can do to help?"

"Just clear our things away, if you would. I'd appreciate it."

"I'm glad to pitch in." Jeanne smiled.

She heard the clatter of hooves outside a moment later, and when she had taken the dirty plates to the big dishpan, she went to the door and looked out. The stage had rocked to a stop in front of the station, raising a cloud of dust that was now blowing off across the little valley.

"Arlo Jenks, you old fool! Good to see you!" Micah called to the driver. "Who's that with you—Fred Barker? Howdy, Fred."

The driver and the shotgun guard returned Micah's

greetings as they swung down off the box of the coach. It was a Concord, one of the proud products of the Abbot-Downing factory, and though it was not new by any means, it was still almost as sturdy and travel-worthy as it had been when it first rolled down the trail to the West.

The driver was a middle-aged man with a pinched face, three days' worth of beard stubble, and a black eyepatch. His clothes were shabby and his expression was sour. But when he paused and patted one of the horses in his team, Jeanne could see a gentleness in him. "Take good care of 'em, Micah," he growled.

"You know I will," the stationmaster growled right back.

The shotgunner, a strapping blond man much younger than the driver, went to the door of the coach and opened it with his left hand. His right still held the shotgun that he normally carried. As he held the door, the passengers began to disembark.

First to leave the stage was a young girl in her early teens. She was pretty, with bright eyes and a frilly bonnet on her mass of brunette curls. As she stepped down to the ground, her gaze darted around the valley, eagerly taking in everything there was to see.

From her position in the doorway, Jeanne watched the girl and smiled at the enthusiasm of youth.

Following the girl off the stage was a man in a banker's suit. He was middle-aged, stoutly built, and looked none too happy as he took off his hat and brushed dirt from it. His broad, florid face was set in lines of annoyance. His hair, uncovered at the moment, was salt-and-pepper, though there was more salt than pepper, Jeanne reflected. She thought she could see a resemblance between him and the girl and wondered if they were father and daughter.

The next two people to disembark were a sharp contrast to the dark-suited businessman. They were young women, though nowhere near as young as the girl—perhaps in their late twenties, Jeanne pegged them. One wore a royal-blue dress and had hair dyed a flamboyant shade of red, while the other's hair was a more subdued henna, though definitely not her own. Her dress was equally as

bright as her friend's—a shimmering copper color—and
they each wore a hat with feathers adorning the bands.
When one of them let out a rather loud laugh at a comment from the other, the businessman glanced at them
and then pointedly ignored both.

The final passenger was a man whose unusual height
became apparent as he stepped down to the ground and
unfolded himself. He was tall, but his slenderness made
him seem even taller. His suit was a light tan color, his hat
a dark brown under the inevitable coating of dust. He
wore a narrow mustache a shade darker than his dark-
blond hair.

Jeanne would have been willing to bet that he had a
gun hidden somewhere on him. She immediately recognized his type, having seen enough professional gamblers
to pick them out on sight. Yet there was something vaguely
familiar about this particular man, and she wondered if he
had come into the Black Bull while she was there. After
all, this stage had come from Albuquerque.

For a moment the thought occurred to her that the
gambler might be one of Landreth's men, sent out to look
for her, but as he walked toward the building, his eyes
passed over her quickly, paying little attention to her. If
he was working for Landreth, changing her appearance
had worked. The most effective disguises were sometimes
the simplest, Jeanne knew.

She stepped out of the doorway to let the passengers
from the stage file into the station. Alice greeted them by
saying, "Howdy, folks. Have a seat at the table, and I'll
bring your food."

Jeanne pitched in without asking again, taking two of
the plates from Alice and carrying them to the table. She
set them down in front of the middle-aged man and the
young girl. As she did so, she felt eyes on her and glanced
up to meet the gaze of the gambler. When she did, he just
smiled thinly, nodded, and then looked away, already
losing interest.

Jeanne knew she looked rather mousy at the moment.
That was the way she wanted it.

Alice served the other three passengers, and all of
them fell to eating with enthusiasm. The stage had left

Albuquerque early in the morning, and it had been a long time since breakfast. A few minutes later, the driver and the guard came in, accompanied by Micah Donahue. The driver saw Jeanne carrying the coffeepot to the table and asked, "You take on some new help, Micah?"

"She's a passenger, Arlo. It's just that some people like to be helpful, rather than being argumentative old goats."

"Argumentative, am I?" Arlo demanded harshly. "Why, you—"

The guard laughed at the banter and sank down on one of the benches beside the table. He grinned at Jeanne and said, "Do you believe it? I have to listen to this every time we stop here at Slick Rock Station."

Jeanne returned his smile and sat down a few feet away on the same bench. "I'm sure they don't mean it," she said as Alice brought plates for the driver and the guard.

"Heck, no, they don't mean it. But I still get tired of having to listen to them go at each other."

"We can transfer you to another run, boy," the driver growled as he sat down.

The guard shook his head. "Not now, Arlo. Not after I'm just getting used to it. Anyway, it wouldn't be fair to whoever got stuck with you."

No one lingered over their meals, and conversation was kept to a minimum. The stage had a schedule to keep, and the passengers were eager to get to their destinations. Still, there was some talk, and Jeanne listened to it carefully. She thought about trying to draw out the passengers and find out more about them, but that did not seem an appropriate action for the shy personality she had adopted.

She managed to learn that the businessman's name was Benjamin Kimbrough and the girl was his daughter Marjorie. The gambler was called Forrest, but Jeanne was not sure if that was his first name or last. The two flashily dressed young women were Roseanne and Casey, and they seemed to be enjoying the journey more than any of the others. Jeanne had a pretty good idea from their clothes and the heavy makeup they wore that they were what polite society referred to as soiled doves. They seemed well acquainted with Forrest, though he resisted their efforts to include him in their joking. That was natural enough; gamblers and prostitutes often knew each other, since they all made their livings in saloons.

"There was that stage trip we took from Fort Worth to Austin, remember, Casey?" the one with the more subdued red hair was saying. "Remember that whiskey drummer?" She arched her eyebrows and giggled, and the flame-haired Casey joined in the laughter.

"I remember what he said to the Bible salesman!" Casey chortled. "I thought the little fella was going to shrivel up and die right there!"

Jeanne saw that Marjorie Kimbrough was hanging on to every word that Roseanne and Casey said, obviously fascinated by them. Marjorie ignored the stern looks of warning that her father gave her.

As soon as the driver had cleaned his plate, he pushed away from the table and stood. "Time's a-wasting, folks," Arlo said. "We'd best get rolling again." He turned to Jeanne. "Micah said you was going to be riding with us."

"I ain't wrote up her ticket yet, Arlo," Micah said. "I'll do that right now. She's already paid me."

Arlo nodded. "All right. Got any baggage, ma'am?"

"I . . . I'm afraid not," Jeanne said.

The conversation around the table quieted. Even the poorest cowhand usually had some kind of baggage, even if it was only a small satchel in which to carry his belongings.

"Jeanne lost it when her horse ran away," Alice suddenly said. She wanted to spare Jeanne the embarrassment of repeating the story of how she had run away from Albuquerque. Jeanne gave her a glance of gratitude, a little surprised that Alice had come up with a little embellishing of her own.

"That's right," she said softly. "I just had enough to purchase my ticket to return home."

"Well, don't worry about it none," Arlo said gruffly. "Lots of folks out here got less than that." He went out, followed closely by shotgunner Fred Barker.

The new team was already in place, so all that remained was for the passengers to board the stage again.

The Kimbroughs were the first ones to climb into it, just as they had been first to get out. Roseanne and Casey followed, but Forrest stepped back and swept off his hat. "After you, ma'am," he said to Jeanne.

Holding the edge of the door, she pulled herself up into the coach. Kimbrough and Marjorie were already in the rear seat, facing forward, while the two prostitutes were sitting across from them. Jeanne started to sit next to Kimbrough but gave in to an impulse and settled down next to Roseanne. The henna-haired woman looked surprised. She had probably expected Forrest to sit next to her, though she did not seem to mind Jeanne's presence.

Forrest climbed into the coach and sat next to Benjamin Kimbrough. Outside, Fred had already climbed up on the box and was resting the shotgun across his knees. Micah came out of the station holding a piece of paper, which he handed to Arlo Jenks. "There's Jeanne's ticket," Micah said. "You take good care of her, you hear?"

"I take good care of all of my passengers," Arlo said with a glower. He reached up for a hold and hauled himself onto the box.

Jeanne looked out the window and saw Micah and Alice standing in the yard of the station. They smiled at her and lifted their hands to wave a farewell. Just then, Arlo Jenks took up the whip and popped it over the backs of the team, yelling as the coach lurched into motion. As it rolled away from Slick Rock Station, Jeanne returned the waves of the couple she was leaving behind. Micah and Alice had been good to her, and what they had done had been out of the kindness of their hearts. Jeanne wished she could run into more people like that, instead of murderous snakes like Darryl Landreth.

Roseanne and Casey kept up their chattering as the stage put the miles behind it. It had been a while since Jeanne had ridden in a coach, and her stomach rebelled slightly at the constant rocking motion. She got used to it, to a certain extent, and tried to keep her mind off her stomach by concentrating on her fellow passengers.

To hear Roseanne and Casey tell it, they had been practically everywhere in the West, from the Rio Grande to Montana, from the Great Plains across the Rockies to the Pacific. That was possible, Jeanne supposed. Women in their profession—much like the few women in Jeanne's—tended to move around a lot.

Marjorie Kimbrough was still listening intently to what they had to say, occasionally asking them a question that would set them off on another series of anecdotes. Marjorie's father glared at her every time she spoke to the two soiled doves, but the girl paid little attention to his disapproval.

After a long, slightly ribald story about their adventures in the Black Hills of South Dakota, Marjorie leaned forward and asked breathlessly, "Weren't you scared, traveling alone like that through Indian country?"

Casey laughed. "We weren't alone for long, dearie. A gentleman came along and took us under his wing, I guess you could say. Gentlemen always come along just when you need them, like Lloyd here. He's an old friend of ours, aren't you, Lloyd?"

"An acquaintance would perhaps be a better way to describe our relationship," Forrest said. Jeanne thought his tone was a bit rude, but the two women seemed not to notice. "We're hardly traveling together."

"We're on the same stage, ain't we?" Roseanne asked.

"As fellow passengers, nothing more."

The two women finally looked somewhat offended, pouting in response to Forrest's comments. That lasted less than a minute, however, and then they were once more regaling Marjorie with an unlikely story about the time they had met General Custer, before his unfortunate encounter on the Little Big Horn.

Jeanne looked out the window and tried not to smile. She knew that Roseanne and Casey were making up their stories as they went along, but she could hardly fault them for lying. Maybe that was one way they were able to ignore the often squalid reality of their lives. For that matter, Jeanne herself was an accomplished fabricator, as she had proven at the stage station with the yarn she had spun for Micah and Alice.

Jeanne felt someone watching her and looked across the coach to see Benjamin Kimbrough regarding her with polite interest. "Might I ask your destination?" he asked.

"I'm going to Denver," Jeanne said. She doubted that Kimbrough was really interested in her; he probably just wanted to start a conversation to compete with the bawdy recollections coming from the two prostitutes.

"Wonderful city, Denver. Is this trip for just pleasure, or are you tending to family matters?"

"I'm going to meet my fiancé," Jeanne told him, sticking to her story.

"Pleasure, then." Kimbrough smiled, but the expression did not reach his small eyes. "At least let us hope so."

"Yes," Jeanne agreed.

Roseanne paused in the story she was recounting to Marjorie and glanced over at Jeanne, frowning thoughtfully. After a moment, she said, "You know, sweetie, you could be pretty good-looking if you'd just fix yourself up."

"That's right," Casey put in. "We could do wonders for you."

Jeanne tried to look embarrassed. She started to awkwardly say thanks, but Roseanne waved it off.

"No, I mean it," she said. "Take that dress you've got on . . ."

Kimbrough spoke up. "There's nothing wrong with the young lady's dress. A little decorum never hurt anyone."

"Neither did a little of something else, mister," Casey snapped back. "That dress is so drab, and it covers everything up." She shook her head and said to Jeanne, "You've got a lot to learn, honey, and we could teach you."

"I-I'm sure you could," Jeanne said, "but I'm only going to Denver."

"Plenty of time," Roseanne assured her. "We'll make a new woman out of you. What do you think, Lloyd?" She looked across the coach at the gambler.

Forrest studied Jeanne with that slightly mocking half smile on his lean face. He seemed to be paying close attention to her for the first time. Finally, he said, "I think the lady could be quite lovely. If I may be so bold, I must say I'd like to see that red hair of yours unpinned."

His eyes were fixed on Jeanne, and the blush she felt creeping over her was the real thing, not part of her pose. He was apparently an insolent, arrogant man.

"Could you help me like you're going to help Jeanne?"

Marjorie asked excitedly, ignoring her father as he snorted in surprise.

"Maybe in a few years, kid," Casey told her.

"You'll do no such thing!" Kimbrough exclaimed.

"Take it easy," Roseanne said. "We're not going to corrupt her or anything."

Jeanne wished the conversation had not taken this turn. She did not want attention focused on her, especially not on her hair.

"Yes, you do have the loveliest red hair," Forrest murmured as if reading her mind, and Jeanne felt her heartbeat increase. Had he recognized her? Did he know that Darryl Landreth was looking for her?

She should have dyed that red hair of hers a long time ago, Jeanne thought now. She was not sure why she had not. Pride, perhaps—pride in the appearance that nature had given her.

Pride could be dangerous. Jeanne only hoped it was not going to get her killed.

Chapter Five

During the previous night, Stuart Davis made the grim ride from his father's way station south into Santa Fe, leading the horses of the four outlaws who had come to the station. The two dead men were slung over their saddles and tied on, while the two who were still alive rode, though they were securely trussed up. If there was one thing Stuart had learned during his years as a marshal, it was how to handle prisoners.

"I'll remember you, mister," one of the prisoners snarled as the little group entered Santa Fe several hours later. He was particularly angry, since he had had the hot water dumped on him, and much of his face was reddened and puffy, with a few blisters on the cheeks. "One of these days you'll get what's comin' to you!"

"You're probably right," Stuart said mildly. "People usually get what's coming to them."

And most of the time it's bad, he added to himself.

Still, a man could not complain too much about his surroundings, not in this part of the country. In spite of the violence of the night before and the grim errand he now was on, Stuart could not help but be impressed by the crisp predawn air that carried a hint of coldness in it, even though it was summer.

It was good country, Stuart mused. Country worth staying in, instead of running around all over the West as a deputy U.S. marshal, plunging into whatever hellhole the government wanted him to tame. Yes, it was time for him to settle down, he reflected, trying to convince himself that the stage holdup had nothing to do with his decision.

As he reined up in front of the Santa Fe sheriff's office, the night deputy who was sitting on the porch looked up at him in surprise. The man was leaning against the wall in a cane-bottomed chair, and its legs came down with a thump as he sat up.

"Howdy, Stuart," he said as he took in the spectacle of the two prisoners and the matching number of corpses, illuminated by the light of the street lamp. "What you got there?"

"Just some business for Ben," Stuart answered. "When will he arrive?"

"Just after sunrise. Why don't you bring the live ones inside. We'll lock 'em up and heat up a pot of coffee. Won't be that much longer until Ben's here."

Stuart and the deputy ushered the two prisoners into the jail and soon had them locked up in the cellblock behind the sheriff's office. As the deputy slammed the heavy metal door leading into the cellblock, the two men cursed loudly at Stuart.

"Sounds like those boys ain't too fond of you, Stuart," he said dryly.

"I'd say you're right," Stuart agreed. Cuffing his hat to the back of his head, he went over to the coffeepot warming on the cook stove and helped himself to a cup of the strong black brew. The two men sat and, sipping coffee, caught up on the local news as the sun rose.

It was not long afterward that Sheriff Ben Crider stepped up onto the porch and opened the door to the office. Crider was a stocky, middle-aged man, not a fast gun by any means but nevertheless a tough, respected lawman.

Crider stopped at the sight of Stuart. "You and George have some trouble out at the station? I saw the bodies outside," he said and then walked inside and shut the door.

Stuart nodded. "Those two gents and their two friends in the cellblock rode in last night looking for a drink and something to eat. They started a ruckus when one of them recognized me as a marshal."

"Wanted, eh?" Crider opened the door to the cell-block and disappeared for a few moments. When he returned, he said, "They look familiar, all right. We'll find 'em when we go through the reward posters." He glanced over at his deputy. "You go down to the undertaker's and get Farley up here to take care of them other two."

"You bet, Ben," the deputy said, hurrying down the street to bring the local undertaker.

"It looked like you handled the other two without much trouble."

Stuart stretched and yawned. "They didn't give me much choice. You going to hold an inquest?"

"Reckon we ought to. It won't be anything but a formality, though." Crider sat down at his desk and pulled out a stack of wanted posters, riffling through them until he found the ones he wanted. He spread the two posters out on the cluttered desktop. "That's them, all right. Couple of hardcases named Estleman and Sherman. Thought I recognized 'em."

Stuart moved over to look at the reward posters. He reached down and thumbed through the stack, pulling out a couple of more sheets. "These are the other ones."

Crider nodded. He did some calculating in his head and then said, "Looks to me like you got about fifteen hundred dollars coming for these boys, all told."

Stuart shook his head. "I'm not interested in reward money."

"But you've got it coming."

"Marshals aren't allowed to keep reward money. You know that, Ben."

Crider looked thoughtfully at Stuart. "I didn't know if you were going to go back to being a marshal or not. Besides, you're on a leave of absence, ain't you? Way I see it, you're entitled to that money."

Stuart drained the coffee and put his cup down on the desk. "Sorry, Ben. Maybe I could claim it, but I just don't want it."

"Suppose that's up to you." Crider shrugged. He paused and then asked point-blank, "*Are* you going back to the marshal's office?"

Stuart was looking at the gun rack on the wall where

several Winchesters were kept. He did not glance at Crider as he said, "I don't know. I'm thinking maybe I won't."

The sheriff leaned forward. "If you don't," he said, unable to keep the eagerness out of his voice, "I could sure use a good man around here. You keep that in mind if you decide not to go back to Uncle Sam."

Slowly Stuart shook his head. He smiled slightly as he said, "I think I've about had my fill of wearing a star. My dad can always use my help out at the way station. And he can't keep running the place forever."

Crider snorted. "I'm not so sure about that. I've known George for a lot of years, and he don't seem to get any older."

"Just more crotchety."

Crider laughed. "Danged if that ain't right." His face became more serious as he went on, "Anyway, you remember what I said."

"I'll remember," Stuart promised. "But don't count on me." He went to the door of the office, stopped, and glanced over his shoulder. "Let me know about the inquest."

"I'll do that." Crider nodded.

Stuart left the office and went down the street to get some breakfast at a café. Then he untied his horse, mounted up, and pointed the animal south once again. It would take him until noon to return to the station; he would have plenty of time to think about what Crider had said. Plenty of time for all the memories to come back again. . . .

Time seemed to slow for Jeanne Townsend as she rode the stage north toward Santa Fe. She knew it was only because she was anxious about possible pursuit from Darryl Landreth, but the knowledge did not do anything to relieve the tension building within her. She should have been enjoying the magnificent scenery through which the coach was passing—snow-topped mountains, pine-covered hills, valleys carpeted in lush green grass. Even the more arid areas, where the vegetation was sparse, had a kind of craggy beauty about them. Yet despite the fact that Jeanne spent a lot of time looking out the window, she did not really see the landscape.

Thankfully, Roseanne and Casey had dropped the

subject of changing the way she looked, and no more mention had been made of her red hair. Forrest seemed to be paying no attention to her now, and Jeanne was grateful for that. It was starting to look as if she had suspected him needlessly.

Benjamin Kimbrough talked to her occasionally; he seemed to regard her as the only passenger worthy of his conversation, aside from his daughter. She learned that he was a businessman, as she had suspected, and owned several mercantile stores scattered through the territory. His home and office were in Albuquerque, but he had to make occasional trips to the other stores to make certain that they were being run properly. On this trip he was on his way to his Taos store, where he would spend several days checking the account books there while Marjorie was visiting her older, married sister.

Jeanne did not do much to encourage the conversation, but that did not stop Kimbrough. At the same time, the two soiled doves were still talking, so the interior of the coach got noisy at times. Jeanne wished they would all shut up and leave her alone, and from Lloyd Forrest's expression, the gambler shared her sentiments.

There was a brief stop at midafternoon as the team was changed at another way station. Jeanne was pleased to be able to get out and stretch her legs and enjoy the faint breeze. As she had suspected, the woolen dress had proved to be extremely hot and itchy.

While the teams were being changed, Jeanne went up to Arlo Jenks and asked, "Will we be stopping for supper in Santa Fe?"

Arlo shook his head. He did not look at her but instead kept a habitual glare on his face as he watched the hostlers working with the horses. "Get there too early for that," he said shortly. "Meal stop's farther on at the next station."

"We do stop in Santa Fe, though, don't we?"

"Long enough to change horses. Ten or fifteen minutes."

Arlo's voice sounded slightly annoyed as he answered her questions. She nodded, said, "Thank you," and walked toward the coach.

"You seem anxious to get to Santa Fe," a voice said beside her.

Jeanne glanced over to meet the level gaze of Lloyd Forrest. He was regarding her with interest, evidently having overheard her conversation with the stage driver. "I was just curious," she said.

"I see. Well, if there's any way I can help satisfy your curiosity about anything, just let me know."

"I'll do that."

Jeanne did not have to fake her look of confusion as Forrest smiled at her and moved away. Her suspicions of him came back. But if he was working for Landreth, why hadn't he made a move before now? Maybe he was not sure of her identity and was waiting for something to confirm it.

In any case, Santa Fe could not arrive too soon for Jeanne. Once the coach reached the city, she could send a wire to Denver. That way, if anything happened to her, someone else from the agency could step in and put a stop to whatever scheme Landreth was hatching.

As she stood beside the coach, waiting for the order to reboard, she glanced over and saw that Forrest was watching her. And he was making no effort to be inconspicuous about his scrutiny, either. When their eyes met, he merely smiled and nodded. Jeanne quickly looked away, her brow furrowing in a frown.

Standing across the way, Lloyd Forrest wished he could remember where he had seen the redhaired woman before. She was quite a mystery. He had paid little attention to her until Roseanne and Casey had pointed out that she could be attractive if only she tried. After due consideration of the matter, Forrest had to admit that the two strumpets were correct. Jeanne would be beautiful . . . if only she would not try so hard not to be.

Forrest was certain he had seen her somewhere before. He could not remember where or what the circumstances had been, but he had a good memory for faces and knew that he had seen Jeanne's. His memory rarely played tricks on him—neither with faces nor with the cards in his hand.

Forrest was in his early thirties, though he was well aware that he looked older. Years of all-night poker games followed by breakfasts of rye whiskey did that to a man. He had chosen the way he wanted to live, however, and did not feel he had any right to complain. There were hardships, of course, but none to compare with the bleak existence he could have had on a hard-scrabble farm back in Kansas. His older brother was still back there on the family farm, and Forrest marveled that he had not already worked himself to death.

Though he was still looking at Jeanne, Forrest's mind strayed back to the days before he ran away from the farm, days nearly fifteen years past. He had been almost nineteen and had been in love—or at least had thought that he was—with a young woman named Marion Wilson, the only child of a prosperous merchant.

Marion had no doubts that she and Forrest would be married and would live a comfortable life in town, where her father had offered Forrest a job at his mercantile store, with the understanding that one day the business would be turned over to the young couple. But Forrest had always had a streak of wanderlust, and though he genuinely cared about Marion, he had trouble envisioning himself spending his life behind a store counter. In the end, he had decided to travel for a year before settling down. But that year had stretched to two, and finally Marion had written to say that she had met another man and that they were marrying.

Over the years, Forrest had never really regretted his decision—except on occasion when life on the road seemed too long and lonely. Yet even then he had known he would not have lasted long in the life Marion had planned for him. Now, fifteen years later, he was no longer so sure.

Forrest had recently received a letter from his brother, in which he had learned that during the past year Marion's husband had died. Since her father had died five years earlier, she now was sole owner of the thriving mercantile business. Apparently she had never forgotten Forrest, for on several occasions since her husband's death she had inquired about him and had asked his brother to send her regards the next time he was in touch with Forrest. Along with those regards was an invitation to call on her the next time he was in the area.

As the road grew harder and the days and nights longer and lonelier, Forrest found himself wondering if perhaps the time had come to settle down—if perhaps calling on Marion might be a good idea, indeed. So he had booked himself on a stage that would take him to Denver and then on to Kansas.

As Forrest stared across the aisle at Jeanne, he realized part of why she seemed so attractive to him. She reminded him somewhat of Marion—the kind of steady, level-headed woman with whom a man could settle down and make a home. Yet there was something else about Jeanne—some inner fire that seemed on the verge of erupting—which intrigued him perhaps even more. As he began to muse about the qualities that attracted him to a woman, the touch of a hand on his arm brought him out of his reverie.

"That little mouse ain't enough woman for you, Lloyd, honey," Casey said from beside him. She stepped closer and leaned into him, letting him feel the soft warm swell of her breasts against his arm. "You need more of a woman."

"That's right," Roseanne said. She was on his other side, and she took that arm. "It's been a long time since you paid either one of us a visit. Don't you miss us, Lloyd?"

Forrest smiled thinly. "You're both delightful creatures," he told them. "However, I seem to have other things on my mind these days."

"You mean you're getting old?" Casey asked. She laughed. "Not damn likely. Not the Lloyd Forrest I knew back in Amarillo."

Forrest shook them off, losing what little patience he had. "That was a different time," he said shortly. "Things have changed."

Roseanne's face tightened with anger. "Oh, they have, have they? You mean to say that you're too good for a couple of whores now, don't you?"

"You said it, my dear, not I."

"Well!"

"I guess we know when we've been insulted, don't we?" Casey added. "Come on, Roseanne. Let's go talk to that shotgun guard. He's a handsome young fellow, not like this dried-up old gambler!"

Forrest watched as the two women flounced away angrily, and he felt a slight pang of regret for having insulted them. He really had nothing against them. He just had other things on his mind these days. It took more to distract him than the overly familiar charms of the likes of Roseanne and Casey. It took someone like Jeanne. She might look like a schoolmarm, but there was much more to her. Of that Lloyd Forrest was certain.

Nearby, as Jeanne was climbing aboard the stage, Benjamin Kimbrough put a hand on her arm and said, "Sit here beside me, my dear."

Jeanne did not see any way of refusing without making a scene, which she did not want. She sank down on the hard seat next to Kimbrough, leaving Forrest to sit with Roseanne and Casey. There was a mocking smile on the gambler's face as he took his place. Casey, who was in the middle, pulled away from him slightly. In fact, Jeanne thought, both of the young women seemed angry at Forrest, and she wondered what had happened between them. But it was none of her business, she realized, and she did not intend to spend a lot of time and energy worrying about it.

At first Jeanne had thought that Kimbrough's interest in her was that of a lecherous, middle-aged man, but as the stage rolled on toward Santa Fe, she changed her opinion. He seemed to be nothing more than friendly—though somewhat pompous and bombastic—as he told her about his family and his business enterprises. He tried to include his daughter in the conversation, but Marjorie was still more interested in talking to Roseanne and Casey.

With Marjorie as an eager audience, Roseanne and Casey got over their hurt feelings and anger at Forrest and went back to discussing their lives and loves on the frontier. While they were talking about the various saloons in which they had worked, Marjorie blurted out, "I've never been in a saloon!" She glanced at her father. "Papa doesn't think it's proper for a young lady to visit such a place."

"I most certainly do not think it is proper," Kimbrough confirmed. "I've never seen a saloon that wasn't a veritable den of iniquity."

"Yeah?" Casey shot back. "How many saloons have you been in, mister?"

Kimbrough was not prepared for that question. He sputtered for a moment and then said, "Enough to know what I'm talking about, young woman."

Casey began hotly, "I don't think you know your a—"

Roseanne shut her up with a hard squeeze on the arm. She knew that Kimbrough already disliked them, and letting Casey insult him in front of his daughter would only increase his hostility and make the rest of the trip that much more unpleasant.

Jeanne gazed out the window for a moment, hiding the smile that tried to creep onto her face. She almost wished that Roseanne had not stopped her companion from speaking her mind. That certainly would have deflated the pompous Mr. Benjamin Kimbrough.

She happened to glance across the coach and saw Forrest watching her again, a similar smile tugging at his thin lips. There was a speculative expression in his eyes, however, as if he was once again trying to remember where he had seen her.

And they had just been talking about saloons, Jeanne realized unhappily. Maybe the conversation had been enough to trigger some memories in Forrest's brain. Maybe he was remembering a certain redheaded blackjack dealer in Albuquerque. . . .

Jeanne tried not to let the sudden tension she felt show on her face. Lloyd Forrest, however, was an expert at reading the expressions of other people. He saw the slight narrowing of Jeanne's eyes and the faint tightening of her jawline. It was clear that something was worrying her. As she looked away from him and stared out the window again, he decided that she was keeping some sort of secret. Furthermore, he was more and more convinced that he had seen her before, but he still could not place her.

She had said that she was going on to Denver, as was he. That would give him the time he needed. Eventually, he would remember who she was, and perhaps that would reveal to him her mysterious secret. It might even result in a financial profit. If there was a way, Lloyd Forrest would find it. As long as it was not *too* dishonorable . . .

Across the aisle, Benjamin Kimbrough sat stiffly with his arms folded across his barrel chest. If there was one thing he could not abide, it was being made sport of, especially by lower-class people—and those two painted jezebels certainly fit into that category. The gambler, too, was laughing behind that suave exterior. Kimbrough tried to hold down the righteous anger he felt; he had to set a good example for Marjorie, after all.

Not that his teachings in the past seemed to have had any effect on her, he mused. The way she was hanging on to every word Roseanne and Casey spoke, one would think that the girl had never had any moral instruction at all. It was his wife's fault, Kimbrough decided, not for the first time. She was entirely too lax with the child.

Kimbrough forced a smile and turned back to Jeanne, determined to continue his conversation with her and not let the others get on his nerves. Jeanne, at least, showed every sign of being a well-bred young lady, the kind of young woman that Marjorie would do well to emulate.

"Well, my dear," he said, "I imagine that once you're married you'll be keeping busy with the duties of a wife and mother."

"Yes, I certainly hope so," Jeanne replied, continuing the fiction. "Up until now, I've just done a little of this and that."

"Haven't we all, sweetie?" Casey said with a laugh.

Jeanne ignored her, except to blush in reaction to the comment. This would be a good chance to lay in some background and perhaps convince Forrest that he was wrong about whatever he was thinking about her.

"I worked in a dry goods store as a clerk," she said to Kimbrough, "and I taught school for a while." If she was going to look like a schoolmarm, she might as well build up that image. She had enough education to make it plausible.

"Really? How interesting." Kimbrough beamed at her. "I almost wish you weren't leaving the territory. I've been looking for a young lady just such as yourself, someone I could hire to tutor Marjorie and teach her the fine art of being a lady."

"I'm sure you can find someone more qualified than myself, Mr. Kimbrough," Jeanne told him, wanting to nip that notion in the bud. Besides, from the look on Marjorie's face, she already had heard this idea of her father's and did not care for it.

"Well, just in case things don't work out—" Kimbrough began, and then he realized that the invitation he was about to give her might be misinterpreted. He swallowed, stammered, and then went on, "I wish you all the best, to be sure."

"Thank you," Jeanne replied softly as she fought back the edgy feeling that was growing inside her. It seemed to be taking forever to get to Santa Fe. She wished she were there, or better still, already at the Pinkerton office in Denver. The papers she was carrying inside her dress felt warm against her skin, but she knew that was just her imagination.

She was well ahead of the pursuit, she told herself. There was nothing to worry about.

Back at Slick Rock Station, Micah Donahue was on his way to the corral several hours after the stage's departure when he saw the riders coming up the stage road from the south. There were eight of them, and even though they were too far away for Micah to distinguish their features, something about them made him uneasy. He started to turn back toward the station building, but the men were coming fast. They swept into the yard of the station, cutting him off from the building.

"Howdy, mister," the man in the lead said. He leaned on the pommel of his saddle and waited for the dust raised by the group's arrival to settle, and then he asked, "Stage from Albuquerque go through here earlier today?"

Micah nodded. "Right on schedule, as usual."

"We're looking for somebody who might've been on it," the man said. "Reckon you could help us?"

Micah's eyes flickered from face to face. All of the riders were lean and hard featured, and as they watched him, he felt a little cold shiver go through him despite the heat of the day. The leader, though his tone was friendly, had the chilliest eyes of the bunch.

And Micah knew, with a flash of intuition, that it was Jeanne they were looking for.

He shook his head. "Stages come and go all the time," he said. " 'Fraid I don't pay much attention to the passengers."

"This is a meal stop, ain't it?" the man asked.

"That's right." Micah nodded.

"Then you should've gotten a good look at the folks on the northbound. If you saw this little lady, you'd remember her. Red hair, good looking, wearing the kind of dress you'd see in a saloon."

"I don't get into town much," Micah said tightly. "Don't recollect the last time I was even in a saloon."

"You don't remember seeing a woman like that on the stage?"

"I told you, mister. I don't pay no attention to the passengers. All I'm concerned with is the horses."

Micah hoped he did not look as nervous as he felt. He knew instinctively that these men meant Jeanne no good. She had been running scared, and it looked as though she had good cause to feel that way. Well, they would get no help from him.

Matt Briggs stared at the old man and tried to decide if he was telling the truth. There was no real reason for the old mossback to lie—unless the woman had slipped him a few coins to misdirect anybody who came looking for her. From the way Landreth had described her sneaky actions, that would not be beyond her.

Briggs and Landreth's other men had searched every available room in Albuquerque after Jeanne's escape, but there had been no sign of her. Then the next day they had fanned out in every direction around the town, but the cheap little thief had somehow eluded them, despite his posting guards at the train depot and the stage-line office. At that point Landreth had ordered Briggs to head north to Taos, where a job of much greater importance had to be carried out two nights later. Briggs was to follow the stage route, keeping an eye out for the Fontanne woman on his way. There was a good chance she had learned too much from rifling Landreth's desk, and Landreth wanted to determine how much she knew and what she might have done with that information. But Briggs was to abandon the search if it was going to interfere with his getting to Taos on time.

"Micah, what's going on?" a woman's voice asked.

Micah looked past the horsemen and saw Alice standing in the doorway of the station. He bit back a curse, wishing she had stayed out of sight until these men had ridden on. Quickly he strode past the horses and went to the station building, feeling the eyes of the men on his back.

"Nothing's goin' on," he told his wife. "Just some folks lookin' for somebody. I told 'em we hadn't seen her."

"Her?"

Matt Briggs reined his horse closer to the doorway. "That's right, ma'am," he said before the old man could answer his wife's question. "Lookin' for a redheaded gal in a green dress who used to work at a saloon in Albuquerque. She might've come through here on the stage earlier today."

Micah looked hard at Alice, trying to make her understand without saying anything. Evidently he got through to her, because she said, "I'm sorry. I don't remember seeing anyone like that."

"You're sure?" Briggs prodded.

"Of course I'm sure, young man." Alice's voice was tart as she answered. "I have an excellent memory."

Briggs felt his patience slipping, but he tightened the rein on his temper. Darryl Landreth wanted this done quietly, if possible, without rousing the countryside. But Landreth did not always understand the problems a man like Briggs faced. He was back in the Black Bull, safe and sound and demanding results from the people who did his dirty work.

It this case, that was not strictly true, Briggs realized. Landreth would no longer be in Albuquerque. More likely he was on the trail somewhere, taking the shortest route north to Taos. At least that was what he had indicated he was going to do while Briggs and the other men were searching for Jeanne Fontanne along the stage route on their way to Taos.

The answers that the two old people were giving were plausible enough, but Briggs's gut told him they were lying. He did not know why they would lie to help out some thieving slut, but that was none of his business. He came to a decision.

Slipping his gun out of its holster, he said, "No offense, folks, but I think my boys and I will have a little look around this place."

The other men followed his lead, either drawing their guns or resting their hands on them.

Micah stared up at Briggs, outrage on his face. "What the hell is this?" he demanded angrily. "You can't just come in here and start wavin' guns around—"

"That's what we're doing, ain't it?" Briggs asked, his voice even colder now. He jerked his head at a couple of his men. "Take a look inside."

Micah slipped an arm around Alice's shoulders. Though she was holding herself stiffly upright and looked every bit as outraged as her husband, he could feel the slight tremble that ran through her body.

"You won't find anything in there, young man," Alice said. "I believe you've taken leave of your senses."

"We'll see," Briggs snapped, all pretense of politeness gone now.

A thought suddenly occurred to Micah, and he felt fear go shooting through him. Jeanne had left the gaudy saloon dress behind when she left, and he did not know what Alice had done with it.

"Here now," he said, stepping forward as the riders dismounted and started toward the door. "This station is stage-line property, and you're goin' to be in a hell of a lot of trouble if you don't just ride out of here."

"Is that so?" The smile on Briggs's lips was contemptuous. "We'll take the chance, old man." When his men hesitated slightly and glanced at him, he nodded curtly.

When one of the men reached out and shoved Micah to the side, Micah angrily cursed and launched a clumsy punch at the man's head. The hardcase stepped aside, easily avoiding the blow, and sank his fist in Micah's belly. Micah grunted and took a step backward as Alice screamed.

The other man shouldered past her, striding into the building, followed closely by his companion. Alice hurried to Micah's side, clutching his arm as he held his stomach.

Micah shrugged off her grip and pushed her behind him. Leaning against the wall of the station was the pitchfork he used to spread hay in the corral. He lunged for it, catching it up and spinning toward Briggs as Alice cried, "Micah! No!"

"Put it down, old man," Briggs hissed, bringing up his gun.

"You get the hell out of here!" Micah ordered, brandishing the fork. "You've got no right—"

Briggs's eyes flickered, "I think you're lying to me, old man."

Micah saw the deadly intensity in those eyes. He yelled to his wife, "Run, Alice!" Then he thrust the pitchfork at the man on the horse.

Briggs jerked back on the reins, pulling his horse into a tight spin. Micah's pitchfork missed its mark, and he went stumbling past the outlaw's horse.

Briggs squeezed the trigger and shot him in the back, the slug driving him facedown on the ground.

Briggs jerked his gun around and lined the barrel on the woman's face, his finger whitening once more on the trigger. He stopped the motion a split-second before the Colt would have blasted again. A small, still-rational part of his brain took over, dispelling the blind rage that had coursed through him a moment before.

His riders were hard men, no doubt of that, but even they might balk at following a man who would shoot down an old woman in cold blood. After all, he had killed the man in self-defense.

"She's not here, Matt!" a voice called from the doorway.

He slid his pistol back in its holster as Alice ran to Micah's side, falling to her knees beside the body and wailing. A muscle in Briggs's face twitched as he looked at his men and said, "The girl's been here, all right. She must be on that stage. We'd best be riding."

One of the other men jerked his head at Alice and Micah. "What about the old man?"

"He said this was stage-line property." Briggs's voice was bleak. "Let the stage line bury him."

He galloped out of the yard, the other men following, and within a minute the sound of their horses' hooves had faded away. All that could be heard in the little clearing was Alice Donahue's sobbing.

Chapter Six

The stage carrying Jeanne Townsend and the five other passengers reached Santa Fe in the late afternoon. The sun was lowering in the western sky, giving a reddish glow to the countryside. As the coach rolled into the bustling old Spanish town, Benjamin Kimbrough said, "It's going to feel good to get off this rattling contraption again."

Jeanne shared his sentiments. The hard wooden seat had made her feel as if she had been in the saddle all day.

Jeanne had been in Santa Fe once before, though it had been a few years ago. If she was remembering the town correctly, the telegraph office was a couple of blocks from the local stage station. The stage line also had an office here at this station.

Kimbrough and Marjorie were the first ones off the stage after it had rocked to a stop in the dusty street in front of the station. Jeanne hung back until Forrest and the two prostitutes had also gotten off. Then she stepped down from the coach, her eyes scanning the street for any sign of trouble. It was entirely possible that Landreth had already gotten word to his friends here to be on the lookout for her. She did not spot any familiar faces, but that did little to reassure her, since her pursuers might not be anyone she would recognize.

The street was full of traffic, with cowboys and businessmen, miners and Mexicans, jamming the sidewalks. She should have felt safer in a crowd, Jeanne thought, but the presence of all these strangers just made her feel more nervous. She spotted the imposing edifice of the territo-

81

rial capitol a few blocks away, and the sight of it reminded her of the letters hidden in her clothes. Somewhere in that building, Governor Lew Wallace was probably working at this very moment, and for a few seconds, Jeanne considered going to him and dumping this whole mess in his lap. It was he who had come into the territory several years earlier and started cleaning up the graft and corruption that had infested the government. Wallace had broken the back of the loose-knit organization known as the Santa Fe Ring, kicking out the officials who had been in the government only for the purpose of lining their own pockets—including the man who had written the mysterious letters to Darryl Landreth.

Jeanne had been surprised at first that Landreth had not destroyed the letters. They were just incriminating enough to be dangerous. But after thinking the matter over, she had come to the conclusion that Landreth had been crafty by saving them. They would make excellent blackmail material later on, especially if the official in question ever returned to a position of power. And stranger things had happened.

She went so far as to take a couple of steps along the sidewalk toward the capitol when she spotted a man leaning on one of the posts supporting the porch. He was watching her with slitted eyes and a calculating look.

One of Landreth's men? Jeanne did not know, but she stopped, letting the crowd on the sidewalk move past her for a moment, hiding her from the man. She turned and stepped into the stage station. There was a big waiting area with several wooden benches, and the stage-line offices were behind a row of counters to the left. As Jeanne walked toward the counters, she glanced through the windows in the front of the building and saw hostlers changing the team on the coach.

The other passengers were also in the station, stretching their legs while the team was changed. Kimbrough was talking to one of the officials from the stage line, no doubt telling him how to run his business, while Marjorie wandered around the room, looking bored as she studied the schedules posted on the walls.

Roseanne and Casey were giggling at some of the

advertisements also posted on the walls and in the process captivating one of the young clerks, who could not seem to take his eyes off them. Lloyd Forrest was standing by himself at one of the windows, looking out at the street and smoking a thin black cigar. He seemed preoccupied about something, and as Jeanne glanced in his direction, she saw him take what looked like a letter out of his pocket and look down at it. The smoke curled around his head as he studied that paper for a long moment. Then he carefully refolded it and put it inside his jacket.

Jeanne looked out the window again, calculating how much longer it would take the hostlers to get the team changed. She did not have much time, and her indecision about what to do had cost her precious minutes. Moving across the waiting room, she headed toward the rear door of the station.

She slipped out the door, hoping no one had noticed her departure, and turned down the alley in the direction that she hoped would take her toward the telegraph office. After she had gone half a block, she went alongside one of the buildings and returned to the street after checking to make sure the man she had seen earlier was no longer in sight.

A few minutes later she hurried into the telegraph office and went directly to the window where a clerk took messages. He barely glanced up at her as she said, "I need to send a telegram."

The clerk shoved a message blank and the stub of a pencil across the counter. Jeanne took the pencil and quickly printed her message with bold strokes. She handed the blank to the clerk.

His eyes scanned the message as he counted the words, a routine he performed dozens of times during a day. Usually, the messages did not really register in his brain; they were just a series of words to be counted, paid for, and transmitted over the wire. This time he went back and read the message a second time, and his brow furrowed in a frown.

"Pinkerton Detective Agency," he muttered, glancing up at the primly dressed young woman standing on the other side of the counter. She did not look like the type to pull a fellow's leg, but . . . "Is this a joke, ma'am?" he asked.

Jeanne shook her head. "It's no joke," she said anxiously, well aware of the time slipping away. Arlo Jenks might wait for a few minutes if she was not back on time, but he would not wait for long. Besides, she did not want the attention that a late arrival at the station would draw. She took the bill she had rolled up in her hand and spread it out on the counter. "Just send the message, please."

The clerk nodded. "Sure, sure. But the charge won't come to that much, ma'am."

Jeanne slid the money across the counter, her intent obvious. "I don't care about that. I just want that telegram to get through."

"You can count on that, ma'am." The bill disappeared; working a telegraph key all day gave a man nimble fingers. "You'll wait for a reply, I suppose."

Jeanne shook her head. "I don't have time." She went to the door of the office and then glanced at the man. "This is very important."

The clerk nodded. "I understand. Don't you worry about a thing."

Don't worry about a thing. Easy to say, Jeanne thought as she left the telegraph office. Not so easy to do. She had a lot to worry about, not the least of which was making it out of New Mexico Territory alive.

Dusk was settling in, and shadows were starting to creep across the street as Jeanne hurried to the stagecoach. She was within a block of the station when a dirty hand came out of a doorway and clamped on her arm, yanking her to a halt. Shocked, she jerked her head around and found herself looking at the man who had been watching her earlier. He was tall and angular, wearing patched range clothes and a dusty, flat-crowned black hat. A cigar dangled from his left hand, and the fingers of his right were digging into Jeanne's arm. She could smell whiskey on his breath as he squinted at her.

"Hold on there, lady," he said. "Want to talk to you."

Jeanne cast her eyes around. There were plenty of people passing by on the sidewalk, but none of them seemed to be paying any attention to what was going on in the doorway. The door itself led into a millinery shop, but it was already closed for the day.

"What do you want?" she demanded, trying to pull away from him.

He only tightened his grip painfully. "I saw you earlier when you got off the stage, lady," he said. "Wanted to talk to you then, but I sort of lost track of you."

She still could not tell if he was one of Landreth's men or not. The eyes watching her were sparkling with a drunken glint, and it was possible that he was just trying to make advances to her.

"Please, I have to get back to the stage before it leaves," she said, trying to reason with him.

"You're a pretty little woman, you know that? I like a gal without a bunch of paint and spangles once in a while."

Jeanne felt a surge of hope. He was just a drunken cowboy, not a hardcase riding for Landreth. She felt confident she could get away from him. The question was whether she could do it in time to catch the stage.

The man leaned forward, pulling her up against him. "All women got the fire in 'em," he mumbled. "Sometimes you just got to fan it a little harder to get it blazin'. You know what I'm sayin', lady?" He grinned crookedly.

Jeanne knew, all right. She knew she was going to have to deal with this lout, even though the most effective method would draw more attention than she liked.

With his whiskey breath blowing in her face, she took a ready stance, bracing herself. The cowboy was about to be mighty surprised. . . .

"Having some trouble, ma'am?"

The soft voice came from behind her. Jeanne glanced over her shoulder and saw Lloyd Forrest standing there, that enigmatic half smile on his narrow face.

"No, the lady's not havin' any trouble," the cowboy answered harshly before Jeanne could say anything. "Why don't you move along, dude?"

Jeanne's eyes met Forrest's. "Is the stage—?"

"About ready to move out," the gambler confirmed. He looked icily at the man holding Jeanne. "Why don't you let the lady go, friend? She's hardly your type."

The cowboy's face, already flushed from drinking, got even more red with anger. "Who the hell are you to tell me what my type is?" he demanded harshly. "She's a woman, ain't she? That's enough for me."

"Let her go." Forrest's voice was low pitched now and taut with menace.

The cowboy thrust Jeanne to the side, shoving her roughly into the wall at the side of the doorway. "You tinhorn son of a bitch!" he snapped, grabbing for the pistol holstered on his hip.

He was surprisingly quick, considering his inebriated condition, but Forrest was quicker. The gambler's hand flickered inside his coat, coming back out with a small .22 caliber revolver. The tip of the little gun's barrel thumped painfully against the cowboy's nose, and then Forrest pressed the gun hard against the man's face, just under his left eye.

"Don't try it," Forrest breathed.

The man had his pistol halfway out of its holster, but he froze as Forrest drove the weapon against his face. His eyes crossed as he stared in horror down at the barrel of the .22. "W-wait a minute, mister!" he croaked.

"Slide your gun back in the holster—slowly!" Forrest told him. "Otherwise you're going to have a third eye, friend."

The man did as Forrest ordered, reholstering the gun with almost comical caution. But there was nothing funny about the situation. As Jeanne leaned against the wall, she saw the tight-drawn lines of Forrest's face and knew that the gambler was very, very close to killing the other man.

"I didn't mean no harm, honest," the cowboy said. Afraid to move his head, he cut his eyes toward Jeanne and went on hurriedly, "I'm sorry, ma'am, I really am." His face was awash with sweat now, the effects of whiskey being purged from him by fear.

"Good," Forrest said softly. "Now, since you've already apologized to the lady, I think you'd best get out of here. Right now!"

The man turned, cringing as if he expected Forrest to shoot him in the back. When nothing happened, he hurried away down the sidewalk, almost breaking into a run as he glanced over his shoulder. Forrest still had the gun lined on him, which made the fellow quicken his pace even more.

When the man had disappeared into the shadows, Forrest lowered the gun but did not replace it in its holster.

"I think you would have killed that man," Jeanne said to him.

"But of course I would have," Forrest replied. He took Jeanne's arm. "Now come along, we still have a coach to catch. I'm sure our driver is getting impatient by now."

Jeanne fell into step beside him on the sidewalk. Up ahead she could see the stagecoach sitting in the street in front of the station, ready to roll. The other passengers were already on board, and as she and Forrest approached, the driver and the shotgun guard came out of the station and climbed onto the box.

"How did you happen to come along and rescue me?" Jeanne asked softly.

"I'm afraid I didn't just happen along. I saw the way that man was looking at you earlier, and I was afraid there would be trouble if you wandered away from the station." Forrest paused for a moment and then went on, "Did you get your telegram sent?"

Jeanne could not help but catch her breath. She had thought that her actions had gone unobserved.

"Don't worry," the tall man with the sandy hair went on without waiting for her answer. "Your business is your own." His smile became more ironic. "I know all about keeping things to oneself."

Jeanne remembered the paper she had seen him looking at in the station and the somewhat pensive mood he had been in ever since she had boarded the coach at Slick Rock Station. Forrest had something on his mind, and it was obviously something he was not prepared to share with anyone else.

"I . . . did what I needed to do," she said. "And thank you for keeping an eye on me."

"My pleasure."

She was almost ready to believe that he had no connection with Darryl Landreth. Almost, but not quite. Being too trusting of anyone could prove to be a very dangerous thing indeed.

"All right, folks, let's get this stage moving," Arlo

Jenks called out to them. Forrest helped Jeanne into the coach, and she sat down beside Benjamin Kimbrough once more. The businessman was casting a surprised look at her, no doubt shocked that she had come walking up arm in arm with Lloyd Forrest. She could see that her status had slipped a notch in Kimbrough's estimation. It was a fact that did not bother her one bit.

There was still a bright red glow in the western sky as the stage pulled out of Santa Fe, heading north. It would make a meal stop in a couple of hours at a way station, and then following that late supper it would continue on to Taos. After Taos, there was a long stretch through northern New Mexico and southern Colorado where there were few towns. The next major city would be Denver.

No new passengers had boarded the stage in Santa Fe, Jeanne saw as she looked around the rocking, bumping coach. That was a bit of an oddity, she supposed, though fewer and fewer people were traveling by stage these days, with the railroads cutting into the stagecoach business throughout an increasing portion of the West.

Jeanne would stay on the stage, now that she had come this far. She had successfully eluded Landreth's inevitable pursuit. From here on out, she had to take things one step at a time—each step taking her one step closer to safety and the destruction of Darryl Landreth's schemes.

If only time did not run out on her first. . . .

The sun had been down about half an hour when Matt Briggs led his men into Santa Fe. He was tired, and that showed in the slight slump of his shoulders as he sat in the saddle. He and his men had had little sleep in the past two days because of their search for Jeanne Fontanne.

But Briggs knew that Darryl Landreth did not care about sleep. All Landreth cared about was results.

Briggs was sure now that Jeanne was not that far ahead of them. The way the old man at the way station had acted told him that much. There was a good chance she was still on the same stage, unless she had gotten off here in Santa Fe. Either way, he would find her, and then he would take her to Landreth, who could do whatever the hell he wanted with the little troublemaker, as far as Briggs was concerned.

Briggs knew that other groups had been sent out from Albuquerque to aid in the search. They would have headed south and west and east, covering all of Landreth's bets, trying to make sure of everything. But he, Briggs, was the one who had picked up the woman's trail, which was why Landreth always counted on him when the chips were down.

He reined up in front of the stage station. Wearily, he turned in the saddle and addressed his men. "Spread out through town," he told them. "You know we're looking for a redheaded girl. There's no telling where she could be. Ask questions, find out if anybody's seen her. Hank, go down to the livery and get us fresh horses. I'll talk to the people here in the station."

He swung down and tied his horse to the hitch rail by the raised sidewalk. As was typical of towns like Santa Fe, with their long Spanish heritage, many of the older buildings were low, flat-roofed adobes; but this section of town was newer and more American, with frame buildings to house the businesses, such as the stage-line office. Briggs went up the two steps onto the sidewalk, crossed it, and pushed through the door into the station. He swung toward the counters where the clerks worked.

Only one man was on duty at the moment, and he looked up from under his eyeshade as Briggs approached. Something about the newcomer made the clerk frown for a moment. The man seemed dangerous somehow, though he did not look that much different from all the other range riders who passed through this station from time to time. Maybe it was the look in his eyes, the clerk thought.

"Howdy," Briggs said.

The clerk nodded. "Evening, mister. Something I can help you with? You want to buy a ticket?"

Briggs shook his head and said, "I need some information."

"That's one reason I'm here." The clerk tried to smile. He was a young man, not overly bright or ambitious and certainly not looking for any sort of trouble.

"Has the northbound stage from Albuquerque been through here this evening?"

"Yes, sir, it sure has." The clerk glanced at the clock on one wall of the waiting area. "Pulled out about forty minutes ago, in fact."

"I'm looking for a woman who might have been on it," Briggs went on bluntly. He was too tired to waste time trying to be subtle, no matter how much Landreth preferred that approach.

"Well, there were several women on that coach, if I remember right," the young man said.

"This one's got red hair."

The clerk could not help but smile. "Yes, sir, there were a couple of redheaded women, all right. I remember them real well."

A couple? Briggs thought with a frown. "I'm looking for one particular woman," he said. "What did the ones here look like?"

"Well, sir, they were right good-looking. Of course, them dresses they was wearing helped quite a bit." The clerk's smile became more of a leer as he winked at Briggs. "They were plenty daring, if you know what I mean."

"I know," Briggs said grimly; he did not expect a saloon girl like Jeanne to be dressed for going to church. "Was one of them wearing a green dress?"

"No, sir," the clerk said, frowning. "One wore blue and the other's dress was the color of a new penny." The clerk lowered his voice and went on in a conspiratorial tone. "You ask me, with them dresses and the way those two were painted up, they were whores."

Briggs frowned. When Jeanne Fontanne had escaped him in Albuquerque, she had been wearing a green dress. He could not see how she would have been able to change clothes; Briggs's men had kept a close watch on her room. But he supposed that the other redheaded woman, whoever she was, could have given Jeanne a dress to wear, perhaps intending to throw him off her trail. Two of them—that was still puzzling Briggs.

It was possible that Jeanne could have made a friend in the time since she had escaped from Albuquerque, Briggs realized. It was even possible that she had run into another woman she knew from before. "They were together?"

"Oh, yeah. They were talking and laughing the whole time they were here, waiting for the stage to change teams."

"Both of them were on the stage when it pulled out?"

"Yes, sir. I watched 'em every inch of their way into the coach."

"What about any other woman who might've come in on the coach?"

The clerk thought for a moment and then said, "There was a girl traveling with her daddy, but she was only about fourteen. Besides, she wasn't a redhead. And I think there was one more woman. . . ."

"You're not sure?" Briggs said sharply.

"Mister, she wasn't nothing special to make a man remember her, not like those other two. This one looked more like a schoolteacher or a preacher's wife."

Briggs shook his head. "That wouldn't be the one I'm looking for, and neither would the kid. Must be one of the other two."

"Why you looking for her, mister?"

Even before the words were out of his mouth, the clerk regretted them. A question like that was poking into another man's business, and that sometimes was not a healthy thing to do.

"Never you mind about that," Briggs said coldly. "All I want to know is if all the passengers went on."

The clerk nodded, anxious to please. "You bet. Nobody got off and stayed off."

"Anybody else get on?"

"No, sir."

"How many on board? Besides the four women, I mean."

"Just a couple of men. The little gal's daddy, like I said, and a tall fellow who looked like a gambler. They're the only ones I saw."

"Reckon the coach has a driver and a guard." It was more of a statement than a question, but the clerk nodded anyway.

"Yes, sir, the usual pair, Arlo Jenks and Fred Barker. Good men."

"Where's the next way station?"

"About ten miles up the line. That's old George Davis's station."

"They'll change teams there?"

"It's a meal stop," the clerk said. "Davis likes to cook, and he likes the extra money. So they'll be there a little while."

Something like a smile touched Briggs's face. "Thanks," he said curtly. "You've been a lot of help."

Then he turned on his heel and stalked out of the station.

The clerk heaved a deep breath of relief. He had been scared the whole time the hard-faced man was in the station. That was why he had babbled on so, telling the man everything he wanted to know. The clerk knew that if his boss had been there to hear what went on, he would be out of a job now. The stage line did not take kindly to employees who gave out details to strangers. But from the look in the man's eyes, the clerk had decided he would rather risk his job than his neck.

Outside, it did not take Briggs long to round up his men. One of them had been in a saloon talking with a local cowboy who had had a run-in with one of the stage passengers. Briggs listened while his man passed along the story, and then he nodded. The gambler sounded as though he could be trouble, all right. They might have problems with him when they tried to take the woman. A lot of those cardsharps fancied themselves gentlemen, and that demanded some sort of honor, defending ladies and the like.

There would not be any trouble that he could not handle, Briggs knew. As he mounted up and led his men down the street and out of Santa Fe, he could almost taste success.

Before this night was over, the redheaded woman called Jeanne was going to be where she belonged. Right in his hands.

Chapter Seven

George Davis had noticed that his son had seemed troubled when he returned from Santa Fe around noon, but he had refrained from asking what was bothering him, figuring that the ride to Santa Fe with the four outlaws—two of them dead—might have stirred up unpleasant memories of the day Corey was killed. Stuart slept until late in the afternoon and was quiet during their supper. When they had finished, George put the food on the stove, keeping it warm for the passengers on the northbound stage, which was due at nine o'clock.

George had been afraid that Stuart would bring more bottles of whiskey with him from Santa Fe, but that had not happened. There was a little bit of liquor left in the one bottle on hand—the one the outlaws had not finished the night before. Stuart did not go near it, however, leaving it untouched in the cabinet.

George left the building to do his night chores, and when he returned, he had his watch out and was gazing at it. "Stage is due in a few minutes," he said to Stuart, who was sitting at the long table smoking his pipe. George pulled back a chair at the other end of the table and sat down. "Ben Crider find out who them fellers was?" he went on, bringing up the subject of the outlaws for the first time since Stuart had returned from Santa Fe.

"All four of them were wanted," Stuart answered. "Ben had posters on all of them." He recited the names from the reward posters, having already mentally filed them away.

93

"They bring any kind of reward?" George asked.

Stuart nodded, not looking at his father. "Fifteen hundred dollars, total. I told the sheriff I didn't want it."

George's eyes widened, and he opened and closed his nearly toothless mouth a couple of times before saying, "Don't want it? Damn, boy, you know how much money fifteen hundred dollars is? Why, of all the—"

"It's blood money," Stuart cut in. "I don't need it."

"Well, what about your poor ol' pa?"

A smile tugged at the corners of Stuart's mouth. "I guess I didn't think about that. You deserve to be paid for the beans you had to waste."

"Not to mention for savin' your life." George's intentions to leave Stuart alone and let him sort things out went by the board. The grizzled stationmaster let his feisty temper loose as he went on, "Don't see why anybody'd turn down perfectly good money just 'cause it come from capturin' some owlhoots. Hell, you done a service to the community by shootin' them fellers. You deserve to be paid for it!"

"I didn't shoot them for the money," Stuart pointed out. "I shot them to save your hide, and mine."

"That ain't the point—" George broke off his argument and cocked his head to listen. "Reckon that'd be the stage comin'. We'll talk about this reward business later."

Stuart was sure of that, and suddenly he wished he had not told his father anything about it. George just could not understand. Stuart was not even sure if he himself understood.

The stage rolled up the trail from the south as Stuart and George came out into the yard to greet its arrival. Stuart recognized the bulky form of Arlo Jenks on the box, and the figure beside Arlo had to be Fred Barker, the usual shotgun guard. Arlo hauled back on the leathers and leaned on the brake, bringing the coach to a halt in the yard of the station.

"Howdy, Arlo," George called up to the driver. "Everything quiet 'tween here and Santa Fe?"

"Quiet as can be," Arlo said as he swung down from the box. "Got a fresh team ready for me?"

"You're stoppin' to eat, ain't you?"

"Reckon so," Arlo growled.

"Then just you go on inside and eat. I'll handle the teams."

Stuart knew that his father could do just that. There was no better man in the territory than George Davis when it came to handling horses. But Stuart wanted to help his father. He knew good and well that he had been far too gloomy this evening, but he had had some thinking to do, and now he had come to his final decision: He was not going back to being a marshal. With that decision made, he felt as if a great weight had been lifted from his shoulders.

Fred Barker opened the door of the coach and stepped back to let the passengers disembark. In the light spilling through the open door of the station, Stuart got a good look at them. Two women were the first off, both of them moving quickly as if they were trying to get in front of someone. They were flashy in their dress and makeup and hair, and Stuart immediately guessed their profession. Getting off the stage behind them were a younger girl and a middle-aged man. The man was conservatively dressed and looked rather put out, and Stuart guessed that the two prostitutes had been trying to annoy him by getting off the stage first. From the expression on his florid face, they had succeeded.

The next passenger to leave the stage was a plain woman in a simple black dress. The only remarkable thing about her was her red hair, and Stuart was willing to bet that not many people even noticed it, since it was pulled up in a severe bun and she carried herself in a way that made her seem to blend in with her surroundings. Furthermore, most attention would be focused on the more flashy women, who also had hair in shades of red—though even to Stuart it was obvious that theirs was dyed, while this woman's was natural.

The last man off the stage was tall and thin and dressed like a gambler. As he got off the stage, his eyes met those of Stuart, who was standing beside the doorway of the station. The glance lasted only an instant, and then the gambler moved past, following the others into the building and not paying any more attention to Stuart.

For a second, though, Stuart had felt the man sizing him up, weighing his capabilities and trying to determine if he was any sort of potential threat. Living on the edge of danger did that to a man, Stuart knew only too well. In fact, he supposed he had been doing exactly the same thing.

Stuart stepped into the station and approached the passengers, who were standing around the long table. "Just have a seat anywhere, folks," he told them. "Food's on the stove, so help yourself."

He went back out as Arlo Jenks and Fred Barker came in. George was unhitching the team on the coach, taking his time since he knew the passengers would take a while to eat. Stuart went over to help him, not saying anything. George glanced over at his son, grunted, and accepted the help.

"Looks like a typical group," George said after a moment. "Nothin' out of the ordinary."

"I didn't like the way that gambler looked at me," Stuart said. "Hope he's not carrying a grudge from some other time."

George squinted at Stuart. "You recollect havin' a run-in with him?"

"Nope." Stuart shook his head. "But that doesn't mean anything. I might've forgotten him."

"Never knew you to forget much of anything that mattered, son—except'n it had to do with reward money."

Stuart grimaced but did not make any reply.

There was still an uneasy silence between father and son when they came into the station building after switching the teams and caring for the tired horses. The passengers had helped themselves to the food, as Stuart had told them, and they seemed to be enjoying it, even though the fare was pretty simple. The businessman and the two soiled doves had the heartiest appetites of the group, judging by the amount of food on their plates. The gambler, on the other hand, was only picking at his food.

George dropped onto one of the benches opposite the driver and the guard and said to Arlo Jenks, "The food suits you, does it?"

"It'll do for something fixed by a toothless old man," Arlo replied with a scowl.

Stuart and Fred Barker shared a quick grin. They had heard it all before. Arlo Jenks fussed and growled with every stationmaster on the line. As for George, it was one of the high points of his week when Arlo brought a stage through. Much like Micah Donahue farther down the line, he regarded the grouchy driver as a worthwhile opponent.

Stuart walked over to the stove, intending to pour a cup of coffee, but the pot was empty when he hefted it. A soft step behind him made him turn around. He moved a little more quickly than he had intended, and the quiet redheaded woman jumped slightly, as if startled.

"I'm sorry," Stuart said hurriedly. "I didn't mean to jerk around like that." Silently, he was cursing the way old habits and instincts did not want to let go of a man.

"Don't worry," the woman said with a shake of her head. "I saw you heading for the coffeepot and wanted to tell you that it's empty. I put some water on to boil, but I don't know where you keep the coffee, or I would have had some more brewing already."

"That's all right." Stuart went to the cabinet and found the jar of ground beans. As he started preparing a fresh pot, he glanced over at the woman, who was still standing nearby. "Something I can help you with?" he asked.

She shook her head. "No, I thought maybe I could help you. I don't mind fixing the coffee."

Stuart smiled slightly. "No need. Old bachelors like my pa and me learn to take care of kitchen chores."

The woman glanced at the table, where George and Arlo Jenks were still carrying on their good-natured wrangling. "That's your father?" she asked.

Stuart nodded. "Name's George Davis. I'm Stuart." He was not quite sure why he was bothering to introduce himself to this woman. She would be getting on the stage again in a little while, and he would never see her again.

She offered her hand. "Glad to meet you, Stuart. I'm Jeanne Townsend."

The water Jeanne had put on the stove was boiling. He scooped some coffee from the bag and dumped it into the pot, using that action to cover his hesitation. It was not often that a woman offered to shake hands with him.

"Pleased to meet you, ma'am," he said, taking her hand for a second. It was cool and smooth, and there was a surprising firmness in her grip.

"Call me Jeanne," she said.

"All right . . . Jeanne."

Stuart felt vaguely embarrassed by the exchange. He had started out thinking that this woman was rather plain, but now as she stood so close to him, he saw that he had been wrong. There was something indefinably attractive about her, something besides the red hair. He could have sworn that he felt the warmth coming from her body, but he told himself it was just the stove's heat that he felt.

He glanced down at the bubbling coffeepot, looked up, and met her eyes. They were green and sharp and intelligent, and they seemed to be sizing him up. The other people around the table were paying no attention to them, and Stuart suddenly felt as if the two of them were alone.

For her part, Jeanne did not know exactly what had drawn her to this man. As soon as she had stepped off the stage and seen him lounging near the doorway of the station, she had sensed that there was something unusual about him. He had seemed at ease, but she saw the way his eyes touched on each of the passengers as they got off the coach. He was appraising them, maybe searching for familiar faces. His right arm hung at his side, seemingly loose and relaxed, but Jeanne noted that his fingers did not stray far from the walnut butt of his Colt.

And the butt of that Colt, she saw now, seemed rather well-polished from use.

She had seen the signs before. Stuart Davis was a man who was ready for trouble, a man who did not trust anyone overmuch. He was accustomed to riding dangerous trails, and that meant one of two things—he was a lawman or an outlaw.

From the looks of things, however, at the moment he was just helping his father around this way station. Jeanne saw the way he favored his left arm and made the logical deduction. He was recovering from a wound or an injury of some sort. She would have been willing to bet money that it was a bullet wound.

Stuart sensed someone else watching him and glanced over his shoulder. The gambler had shoved his plate away and now sat smoking a thin black cigar. His eyes were speculative as he looked at Stuart. Whatever the man was thinking, Stuart hoped he would keep it to himself.

It was not fated to turn out that way. The gambler stood up and sauntered across the room toward the stove. Stuart turned to face him, not wanting the man to come up on his blind side. Jeanne turned, too, putting her back to the stove.

The gambler stopped a few feet away, a half smile playing about his thin lips. "Pardon me, sir," he said to Stuart. "My name is Lloyd Forrest. Unless my memory is playing tricks on me, I believe we've been acquainted elsewhere."

Stuart kept his face impassive, but he felt his heart sink. So often words like that signaled the start of trouble. "I'm sorry," he said levelly, trying to head things off. "I don't recall having met."

Forrest put the cigar back in his mouth, shifted it from one corner to the other. "I'm certain I've seen you before . . . ," he mused.

"I don't think so. I'm sure we've never met."

Jeanne was watching the two men with interest. Forrest seemed convinced of what he was saying, and Stuart's denials were not ringing true. The gambler was perhaps being a little rude to press Stuart this way, but Jeanne wanted to see what was going to happen.

"I was so sure . . . ," Forrest said softly, almost to himself. Abruptly he glanced up, the memory obviously coming back to him. "Fort Worth!" he said. "It was in the White Elephant Saloon that I saw you."

Stuart bit back the urge to groan. It was true that he had been in the White Elephant a few years earlier. He just hoped that Forrest did not remember in detail what had happened there.

Though Stuart was trying to control his reaction, Jeanne saw it and knew that Forrest had remembered correctly and had touched on something that Stuart would just as soon not bring up.

Stuart did not say anything as Forrest went on, "We

didn't actually meet, but I was there the night you came in to get Jake Diehl. You didn't expect him to have three friends backing him up, did you?"

"No," Stuart said quietly, "I didn't."

"I didn't think you'd stand a chance, going up against four men by yourself like that. It took a great deal of courage."

Stuart picked up the coffeepot. "Or stupidity," he said as he poured a cup of the steaming black liquid.

Fred Barker had gotten up from the table and come over to the stove for a refill, and he heard the last part of the conversation. "Four men?" he said. "You went up against four men by yourself, Stuart?"

"And they were top gunhands, too," Forrest said before Stuart could reply.

The others at the table were looking over now, their interest stirred by Barker's loud question. Stuart saw George looking at him, saw the concern on his father's face. Stuart wished Forrest had kept his memories to himself; he had no desire to be reminded of past exploits.

Jeanne could see the discomfort in Stuart's eyes, and for a moment her heart went out to him. This conversation was plainly bothering him.

"I knew you were a marshal, Stuart," Barker said, "but I never knew you did anything like face down four gunmen."

"They were drunk," Stuart said.

"But still fast," Forrest pointed out. Roseanne and Casey got up from the table and moved over behind him, studying Stuart with new interest as the gambler continued his recitation. "Diehl and his friends went for their guns, but Marshal Davis here outdrew them. He dropped one of them before anyone else got off a shot. Diehl missed with his first try, and he didn't get a second. The other two decided they'd rather give up and live."

There was silence in the station as Forrest finished his story. Then Stuart said, "That was a long time ago. I'm not a marshal anymore."

Stuart saw George squint at him as he heard the decision put into words. It was a decision that had been a long time coming, but it was the right one, Stuart thought.

He had seen more than his share of violence. He was ready to put all that behind him.

Forrest smiled at him. "I'm sure there are a great many lawbreakers who would be glad to hear that, Mr. Davis."

"That's no business of mine," Stuart said shortly. He did not like the way they were all looking at him now, as though he were some kind of hero. He had never been a hero, just a man doing his job. Even Jeanne Townsend seemed to be regarding him a little differently now.

The wheels of Jeanne's brain were turning over rapidly. This Stuart Davis seemed to be a very competent man. Most of the U.S. marshals she had run across had been older and definitely good at their jobs. Stuart had to be near the top to go into a saloon and brace four men, even if he had only expected to find one. Most men would have backed out of a situation like that.

She wondered what it would take to get him to come along with her to Denver. Together, they could deliver the evidence against Landreth, she was sure of that.

Jeanne caught herself, realizing that she was on the verge of trusting someone she hardly knew. That was not smart. No matter what Stuart Davis had been in the past, now he was an ex-marshal recuperating from a wound. He would not drop everything to go with her, not unless she told him the whole truth about herself and her mission . . . and maybe not even then. And she was not prepared to tell Stuart—or anyone else—the truth just yet.

Stuart took his coffee cup and moved away from the stove, stepping around Lloyd Forrest and Fred Barker. Roseanne and Casey were still staring at him, and they followed him over to the table. He put his cup down and started to sit, but the two women were suddenly standing on either side of him.

"You sound like you're hell on wheels, honey," Casey purred, resting a hand on his right arm.

"We don't usually get along with lawmen," Roseanne added, leaning close so that Stuart could feel her breasts pressing into his left side. "We could make an exception in your case, though."

Stuart glanced around the room, fighting the unreasonable feelings of panic that these women were somehow able to generate within him. He saw the disapproval on the merchant's face at this brazen display, saw also the avid interest in the eyes of the teenage girl. Lloyd Forrest wore a slightly mocking smile. The gambler may not have known what he was starting when he brought up the story about Jake Diehl and the White Elephant Saloon, but he was amused by the consequences. Fred Barker also seemed to think it was funny the way the prostitutes had flocked to Stuart, but it was clear that he was a little envious, too. Arlo Jenks's face wore a sour expression, but there was nothing unusual about that. And his father, Stuart saw, just looked worried.

Jeanne watched, wondering what Stuart would do next. Her interest was mostly objective, wanting to see how he would extricate himself from this situation, but she felt a little sorry for him, too. He so obviously wanted to be left alone.

"What do you say, Marshal?" Casey prodded. "I reckon we could have us a hell of a time."

Stuart shook his head. "I reckon not." He pushed past the woman, heading for the door of the station. Rude or not, he wanted some air, and he wanted it now. As he swung open the door, the clatter of hoofbeats filled the air as a group of riders galloped into the yard outside.

Stuart frowned. He should have heard the men coming before now. He would have heard them if he had not been so distracted, he thought.

The horsemen had been riding hard, but now they were reining in, swinging down out of the saddles. Inside the station, Jeanne felt her heart begin to thud painfully in her chest. Even before she saw any of them, she knew who they were. She *knew*.

Chapter Eight

Matt Briggs paused at the doorway of the way station, used his hat to knock dust from his clothes, and nodded to Stuart Davis, who was blocking the way. "Howdy," he said.

Stuart returned the greeting. "Evening," he said. His face was calm, his eyes watchful. These riders in the night might be peaceful enough, but they might also mean trouble.

Seeing the caution in Stuart's eyes and wanting to put him at ease, Briggs turned to his men, some of whom were still dismounting. "You fellas wait out here while I talk to the stationmaster." Then he turned to Stuart and said casually, "Is he here?"

Stuart eyed the man for a moment, and once again his training as a lawman came into play. All he had to do was look at these eight men to recognize them as hardcases. They were dressed much like cowboys, but their holsters were thonged down, and the hands of their leader lacked any rope calluses. And in the man's eyes was something of the look of a hungry wolf. Stuart decided that his best course of action was to keep the leader and his men separated until he was sure of their intentions, and so he nodded into the station and moved aside to let him pass. As Briggs entered the building, Stuart stepped back in front of the doorway to make sure the rest of the riders remained outside.

Jeanne had positioned herself in the shadows near the front door, and she called on every ounce of sheer will-power not to show any reaction as Briggs came into the room. She knew her only hope was to carry on as if she had never seen him before. During the week that she had worked in the Black Bull as a dealer, she had not had any direct contact with him, although she had seen him in the saloon several times. With the change in her appearance, she could at least hope that he would not recognize her.

The atmosphere in the room changed immediately as Briggs entered. George squinted at him, wondering what he wanted at this time of night. Lloyd Forrest, like Stuart, was suddenly more alert, on the lookout for some kind of trouble, as were Arlo Jenks and Fred Barker. Any time you ran across strangers in the night, it was good to keep a close eye on them until you were sure of their intentions.

Roseanne and Casey each reacted instinctively, as well. They smiled at the newcomer, holding themselves so that their figures were displayed to good effect.

The only ones who seemed to be paying little attention to the stranger or the men outside were Benjamin Kimbrough and his daughter, Marjorie.

"Somethin' we can do for you?" George asked, moving around the table.

Briggs smiled at him, but the expression lacked any warmth. "You the manager of this station?" he asked.

"That's right."

"I need some food for my men and grain or hay for our horses. Think we could get some?"

"Reckon you can if you can pay," George replied, the tension he felt easing a little.

Matt Briggs's eyes roved around the room, quickly sorting through the people there. He hardly spared a glance for the stout businessman and the little girl. The stagecoach driver and guard were what he had expected: They looked competent enough, but probably not much of a threat against the likes of him and his men. The gambler near the stove might be more trouble; though many of their type were short on courage, they could sneak up on a man and strike ruthlessly. The old man Briggs dismissed as just another codger running a way station. The younger man at the door, however, would bear some watching.

The women drew most of his interest. There was one

standing in the shadows across the room, not far from the front door. Briggs studied her for a few seconds, but from the severe way she was dressed, he quickly dismissed her, his attention being drawn instead to the two women near the table. They were much more the type to have been dealing blackjack at the Black Bull.

Just as the clerk in Santa Fe had said, they both had red hair, one a more subdued shade. Both wore low-cut gowns that revealed the tops of their breasts, and while neither of the gowns was green, Briggs felt certain that one of these woman was Jeanne Fontanne. Her friend had no doubt provided another dress to mislead any pursuers. They were saloon girls, all right—just the kind of women that Landreth had working in his place. And one of them, Briggs was convinced, was the one he was looking for.

Remembering that the old man had asked him about paying for food and grain, Briggs jerked his eyes off the two women and said, "We can pay, mister. You just bring on the grub."

"I'll put some more up on the stove." George waved a bony-knuckled hand at the table. "You're welcome to a seat, but your boys'll have to wait outside a few minutes until these folks leave." He walked over to the stove to stir the food in the big iron pots.

Briggs masked a slight frown as he mulled what approach to take to get his men into the room. He glanced at the open door and saw that several of the men were standing just beyond the young man who was blocking the way. Confident that they would join in when Briggs made his move, he sauntered over to where Roseanne and Casey were standing. They looked at him blankly as he said, "Hello, ladies."

"Hello, yourself," Casey replied.

"I certainly didn't expect to find two such charming young women out here in the middle of nowhere," Briggs went on. "Coming up from Albuquerque, are you?"

"We're going to Denver," Roseanne said. "You ever get up to Denver, mister?"

"Now and then," Briggs replied. He noted the marks of dissolution around her eyes that even the heavy powder and paint could not completely conceal. He was sure that one of these women was the one he was looking for. And whichever one it was, he had to give her credit for one thing: She had never once cracked under the strain of being on the run. But now that she had a friend, Briggs was afraid that whatever knowledge she had gained by going through Landreth's desk might no longer be her secret. It was clear what he would have to do—bring both of them to Landreth in Taos.

Across the room, Jeanne saw the way Briggs was looking at the two women and knew with a sudden surge of panic what he was thinking. When he had looked her over and then so obviously dismissed her, she had thought that maybe her disguise was going to work. Maybe he and his men would let them leave without causing any trouble to these innocent people. But then he had gone over to the two prostitutes and started talking to them, gazing at their red hair. Jeanne had to stifle a gasp as she realized that he thought one of them was the woman he was looking for.

Jeanne's hopes for no trouble were shattered completely when Briggs suddenly nodded toward the doorway and then swung back to Roseanne and Casey. His hand flickered to his holster, smoothly drawing his pistol and lining it on the two women.

Stuart drew his own revolver, but Briggs had already pulled Roseanne in front of him and had his gun at her head. "Drop it!" he yelled at Stuart, who hesitated but then heard the click of guns being cocked behind him. He did not have to turn his head to realize that the men outside had him covered. Even so, a part of Stuart was crying out with the need to pull the trigger and start blasting. But he knew that if he started shooting, the only possible result would be a massacre. There were just too damned many of the gunmen, and he was sure they would not hesitate to cut down innocent people. Reluctantly, he lowered his hand and let the gun drop to the floor.

He glanced at Lloyd Forrest and then at the driver and shotgunner. All three men were holding themselves in check, though it was obvious from their expressions that they were feeling the same way as Stuart.

George had been facing the stove when Briggs had

made his move, and as he turned around now, he exclaimed, "What in tarnation—?"

"Shut up, old man!" Briggs rasped, pressing his gun tighter against Roseanne's head. "Everybody just stand still, and maybe nobody'll get hurt."

Just then Stuart was pushed roughly into the room, and Briggs's seven men filed in, their guns drawn as they took up positions around the room.

Briggs pushed Roseanne, and she darted over beside her friend, quivering with fear. "One of you gals must be the one I'm looking for, a dame by the name of Fontanne," he told them. "Don't know which one of you it is, so I'm taking both of you with me."

"No!" Roseanne cried.

"We don't know what you're talking about, mister," Casey added, her voice edged with panic as she stared at the barrel of Briggs's gun. "Neither of us goes by that name. We're just minding our own business and heading for Denver."

Briggs shook his head. "Not anymore, you're not." He waggled the revolver. "Come on, let's go outside. And don't try anything."

Across the room, Jeanne watched with growing horror. Briggs had made up his mind that one of the women was his quarry, and he would not be deterred. If Jeanne let him take them, two innocent women could end up dead. She could not allow that. Not when she was the real cause of their trouble.

The envelope concealed in her dress seemed to burn against Jeanne's skin. If she gave up now, the evidence against Landreth would never reach the authorities, and whatever devious plan he was hatching would probably go unchecked. Logic dictated that Jeanne keep her mouth shut and be grateful that Briggs had made a mistake. But sometimes logic was cruel and heartless. There had to be another way out.

An idea sprang into Jeanne's mind, and her eyes darted to Stuart, standing rigidly a few feet away. He was not looking at her; his eyes were fixed on Matt Briggs. She knew how hard it must be for him to stand by helplessly, since she was feeling the same thing. Suddenly she let out a low moan and stepped toward him, moving quickly but not so fast that a trigger-happy gunman would think she was a threat. Stuart turned toward her, and before he knew what was happening, she was in his arms, burying her face against his chest and shivering with fear.

Automatically, Stuart's arms came up and went around her, hugging her to him. He saw the mocking smile on Briggs's face as the outlaw jeered, "Looks like we scared the little mouse." Then Briggs turned to Roseanne and Casey and once again roughly ordered them outside. The two women were clutching each other now, frozen with terror, and Briggs had to reach out, grab Casey's arm, and jerk her away from the other woman. He shoved her toward the doorway.

Jeanne was dimly aware of the warmth of Stuart's body, the strength of his embrace, as she leaned against him. Her right hand lifted and slid inside her dress. Her left side was turned toward the gunmen, and her movements were smooth and unhurried. The envelope made a tiny crackling noise as she slipped it free, but no one seemed to notice. A second later the envelope was underneath Stuart's coat. Jeanne felt him stiffen as he realized what she was doing, but he clamped his left arm down, holding the papers in place.

"It's all right," he said softly, letting the others think he was just comforting her. He reached up to stroke her hair, suddenly all too aware of its sweet fragrance and the way her body molded against his.

One of the gunmen, a big man with a scarred face, was only a couple of feet away. He had an old Remington pistol lined on Stuart, and now a sneer lifted his lip. "Ain't that sweet?" he mocked as Stuart tried to comfort Jeanne.

Jeanne put her hands against Stuart's chest and pushed away from him. The charade had served its purpose. No matter how much better she had felt while he was holding her, the real goal had been accomplished. Stuart had the evidence against Landreth now, and she sensed that he would keep it hidden and know what to do with it later.

Now she must let Briggs know that he was making a mistake—that she was the woman he was seeking.

She turned away from Stuart and took a step toward Briggs. "You can't do that—" she started to say.

The hardcase standing close by reached out to stop her. "Shut up, bitch!" he growled, catching her arm and shoving her to the side.

Jeanne stumbled off balance and felt herself falling. She flung out an arm to try to catch herself, but there was nothing there to latch onto. She went down, and her head cracked against the heavy bench beside the table. For a split second the room seemed to explode with light, and then it vanished in a wash of darkness.

"Bastard!" Stuart burst out. He quivered with the need to smash his fist into the man's ugly face, but the gunman was already facing him again, covering him with the Remington, his finger white on the trigger.

"Let it go, Hogan," Briggs rapped. "We've got to get back on the trail." He jerked his head toward Roseanne and Casey, who were still resisting, and two of his men holstered their guns and came over to grab the women and pull them toward the door.

Stuart's rage was burning inside him, and his eyes met the outlaw leader's as Briggs started to back toward the door, gun still raised. "I'll remember you, mister," Stuart said firmly.

"You do that," Briggs replied with a cocky grin, clearly not too concerned with Stuart's implied threat.

George Davis spoke up, his voice shaking with anger. "Mister, you don't know who you're talkin' to!" he barked. "Why, my boy here—"

Stuart caught his father's eyes and silenced him with a sharp look. George had been about to tell Briggs that Stuart was a marshal—the last thing Stuart wanted right now. Let Briggs think he had them buffaloed, that they were no threat to him.

"Maybe you're right, old man," Briggs said. "All of you take your guns out, real slow, and put them on the floor."

The men in the room had no choice but to comply. There were too many guns being held on them to do otherwise. When all of the men except Benjamin Kimbrough had placed weapons on the floor, two more of the gunmen gathered them up.

"How about you, mister?" one of the men demanded of Kimbrough, stepping closer and prodding his stomach with the barrel of his gun.

Kimbrough looked up at him with fear showing in his eyes. "I'm unarmed, sir," he said. "I'm a businessman, not a . . . a gunfighter."

"A businessman, huh?" Briggs sneered. "Check him for a money belt."

The gunman poked harder at Kimbrough's stomach. "Yeah, he's got one," he laughed. "Off with it!"

Kimbrough whitened as he unbuttoned his shirt and took off the belt. "You can't—"

"We can, and you'd do well to remember that," the gunman told him.

The other outlaw, his arms loaded with the guns, moved past the table behind Arlo Jenks and Fred Barker. Stuart was watching, and he saw the sudden flare of uncontrolled anger in the stage driver's eyes. Arlo had held it in long enough, and now he thought he saw an opportunity to strike back.

Stuart opened his mouth to yell for Arlo not to try it, but he was too late. Arlo catapulted backward off the bench and slammed into the gunman, whose own weapon was holstered. Both men sprawled to the floor, falling heavily. Arlo scrambled to get his hands on one of the guns as Briggs yelled out a curse and then told his other men to hold their fire. Fred Barker was right behind his partner, driving a fist into the face of the fallen gunman.

Arlo came up on one knee, twisting around, a Colt in his big fist. He tried to turn it toward Briggs, but the outlaw was too fast. The gun in Briggs's hand blasted, the slug smacking into Arlo's chest with a thud. The driver was flung backward by the impact, the pistol falling from his hand.

Briggs fired again, hard on the heels of the first shot, and Fred went down, sprawling on the floor next to his partner. Briggs swung the barrel of his gun around to cover Stuart, while his other men menaced the rest of the passengers.

"Stupid sons of bitches!" Briggs snarled as he glanced at the motionless bodies of Arlo and Fred. "I hope the rest of you got more sense."

Stuart had known this was going to happen as soon as he had seen the wild look in Arlo's eyes. The odds were just too great. The only hope for the rest of them now was not to resist.

The men holding Roseanne and Casey had paused in the doorway when the trouble broke out, but now they resumed hauling the women outside. Both of the prostitutes were wailing now, and Briggs called after them, "Shut up or I'll bust your heads open!" He brandished the Colt in his hand at them, and they fell silent after a series of ragged sniffles.

Briggs was the last man out the door. Within moments the women were on horses, each seated in front of one of his men; each woman had her hands lashed together. As Briggs backed out of the station, Stuart knelt beside Jeanne and began to pat her cheeks in an attempt to revive her. He glanced up and met Briggs's gaze once again, and then the outlaw was gone. A minute later, the sound of galloping hooves filled the clearing and then slowly faded.

Chapter Nine

Stuart tried to put the anger out of his mind and concentrate on Jeanne. As he knelt beside her, he ran his fingers through her hair and over her head, feeling the knot that had come up on her scalp where she had hit the bench. As he touched the lump, she winced, and her eyes began to open slowly.

She blinked, trying to focus on the fuzzy shape leaning over her. Gradually, the shape resolved itself into the face of Stuart Davis, a face etched with lines of concern.

"Are you all right?" he asked, his voice sounding far away.

Jeanne tried to nod, but as she did, a wave of dizziness overtook her. She closed her eyes and waited for the world to stop spinning so crazily.

On the other side of the table, George Davis was bent over Arlo Jenks and Fred Barker, checking their wounds. It took him only a moment to determine that the driver was beyond any help. The hole in Arlo's chest had not bled much, but only because the bullet had cored his heart, immediately stopping the flow of blood through his body.

Barker, on the other hand, was still breathing. As George pulled back his jacket, he saw the wide red stain on the right side of the young man's shirt. The wound was messy, all right, but from the looks of it, the slug had not hit anything vital. If he could just get the wound cleaned and patched up, the shotgunner would probably be all right.

Marjorie Kimbrough, who had watched the whole

violent scene in white-faced silence, was now in her father's arms, sobbing brokenly in reaction to her fear. Kimbrough patted his daughter on the back and spoke to her in a quiet voice, trying to soothe her.

Lloyd Forrest strode across the room and stood beside Stuart, looking worriedly at Jeanne. "Can I do anything to help?" he asked.

Stuart came to his feet. "Keep an eye on her," he said, his face set in bleak lines. "She should be coming around again in a few minutes."

Jeanne was already awake enough to hear Forrest's question and Stuart's answer, but her head hurt too much for her to acknowledge them.

"What are you going to do?" Forrest asked as Stuart turned toward the door.

"See if I can tell which way those bastards went."

There was a lantern hanging on one of the pegs near the door. Stuart snagged its handle and carried it outside, digging out a match from his pocket. He paused to light the lantern, well aware that he was making himself a hell of a target if the outlaw leader had left a man behind to pick off anyone who came out of the station too soon. Stuart was being a little foolhardy, and he knew it. He was also too angry to give a damn.

How much of his anger, he suddenly wondered as he walked across the clearing toward the trees, was due to the fact that the woman named Jeanne had been hurt. The surge of emotion he had felt while she had been in his arms had been totally unexpected. There had been women in his life before, but no one serious. No woman had ever made his heart slam in his chest like a crazed animal trying to get out of a trap.

The wavering light of the lantern was enough for him to see the muddled tracks of the horses. The men had entered the clearing from the south and left heading north toward Taos. The night was quiet, the sound of the horses long since vanished. The moon was due to rise soon, and it would provide enough light for the outlaws to ride with reasonable speed. Stuart looked all around the clearing and along the edge of the trees, hoping that maybe the gunmen had dropped the weapons they had taken from the people in the station. That was hoping for too much, he knew, and he was not surprised that there was no sign of the guns. It was a shame, but it was not enough to stop him from going after them.

When he came back into the station a few minutes later, Jeanne was sitting at the table, rubbing her head with one hand and holding a cup of coffee with the other. Forrest stood attentively behind her.

Someone had thrown a blanket over Arlo's body. On the floor nearby was a puddle of blood that marked the spot where Fred Barker had fallen, but now Barker was stretched out on one of the cots in the corner, still unconscious, his face washed out and haggard. George had the young shotgunner's shirt off and was cleaning away the blood around the wound with a wet cloth. What was left of the bottle of whiskey sat on the floor next to the cot, and Stuart knew that George was going to use the liquor to cleanse the wound.

Stuart paused beside the cot and watched his father working on the wounded man. The bullet had passed all the way through, Stuart saw, and he came to the same conclusion as George: Barring infection, Barker would probably recover fairly quickly.

Stuart wanted to talk to Jeanne, but there was something else he wanted to do first. He went to one of the storage bins on the far wall, opened it, reached inside, and brought out a Winchester rifle and a Smith & Wesson .44 revolver. The pistol felt a little different in his hand from the Colt he was used to, but it would do. He delved into the bin once more and came up with two boxes of ammunition.

Sensing someone beside him, he glanced over to see Lloyd Forrest peering into the bin. There were several other rifles and pistols there, different models that Stuart and George had accumulated over the years. Stuart practiced with all of them, since in his line of work he had often had to make do with weapons that were not his usual ones. At least, that had been the case when he was still a deputy marshal.

"Could I borrow one of those weapons, sir?" Forrest asked, gesturing at the guns. "And purchase some cartridges to go with it?"

"What for?" Stuart asked, though he figured he already knew the answer.

"I intend to go after those blackguards and rescue those two ladies."

Flamboyant though his words might have been, there was undeniable sincerity in the gambler's voice. Stuart opened one of the boxes of shells and began thumbing them into the revolver. "That's what I had in mind," he said.

Forrest held out a hand, and Stuart extended the loaded Smith & Wesson to him. The gambler took it, weighed it, and nodded.

As Stuart picked up a Navy Colt and loaded it, he said to Forrest, "No charge for the bullets." Then he walked over to the table and looked down at Jeanne. "How are you feeling?" he asked.

She nodded, grimacing slightly. "A lot better," she said. "It was just a crack on the head. I've been hurt worse."

He studied her eyes. They looked normal enough, and she seemed perfectly coherent.

Jeanne's head was pounding painfully, but she knew she had not suffered any permanent damage from the injury. She would not want to wear a hat for a few days, not with the lump she was sporting, but that was about the extent of it. She sure as hell was not going to let it stop her from doing what she had to do.

"You're going after them, aren't you?" she asked quietly.

Stuart nodded. "Reckon I am."

Jeanne smiled. It was not his fight, she thought, but still he was ready to go out and risk his life getting involved in it. It had not been the prostitutes' fight, either, but they were out there somewhere in the night in grave danger.

Stuart looked over at Benjamin Kimbrough. "What about you, mister?" he asked.

Kimbrough glanced up in surprise. "What about me?" he asked.

"You going with us?"

"What—why—" Kimbrough sputtered. After a moment, he said, "Naturally, I want my money back, but as I told that horrible man, I'm no gunfighter, sir. I'm just a simple merchant."

Marjorie lifted her tear-streaked face. "You've got to go after them, Pa!" she exclaimed. "They took Roseanne and Casey!"

"But that has nothing to do with us, child."

"They're my friends!" Marjorie wailed. "You've got to help them!"

Kimbrough flushed, looking panicky. He hardly thought of the two whores as friends of his daughter, but she evidently did. "I . . . I should stay here to look after things," he said weakly.

"The stationmaster can do that," Forrest put in, annoyed at the businessman's lack of backbone.

George looked up from his task of bandaging Fred Barker's side with strips of cloth. "I'm goin' with you boys," he declared. "You ain't makin' me stay behind. I want to see that damn sidewinder again over the sights of a gun!"

"Somebody's got to stay here," Stuart told him. "There are women to look after, and somebody's got to take care of Fred. Besides, you can't leave the station unattended, and you know it."

"Reckon you're right," George grumbled. "But that don't mean I have to like it."

Stuart glanced again at Kimbrough. "What about it?"

The merchant took a deep breath. "I don't seem to have much choice, do I? I'll come along, though I'm not sure about the advisability of this whole enterprise. It seems to me we should let the law handle it."

"That bunch could be a long way off before we rounded up a posse," Stuart told him. "Can you use a handgun?"

Kimbrough stood up and came over to the storage bin. "I'm a better shot with a rifle," he said.

Stuart took out an older model Henry hunting rifle and handed it to him. "That's the only other spare we've got."

Kimbrough nodded, hefting the rifle somewhat awkwardly. "I can use it," he said. He looked over at his daughter and saw that she looked pleased with his decision. But rather than realizing she might be proud of him, he felt a pang of bitterness that she seemed to care more for the welfare of those two prostitutes than she did for her own father.

Stuart hoped he was not making a mistake taking Kimbrough along. The businessman would probably drag his feet and complain every step of the way, and he might prove to be more of a liability than an asset. With the odds so high against him and Forrest, however, an extra gun was worth the risk.

A voice behind him said, "I'll need one of those guns, too."

Stuart turned around and frowned at Jeanne. "What did you say?"

She held out her hand, palm up. "I said I'll need one of those guns. I'm coming with you."

"The hell you are!" The exclamation was out of Stuart's mouth before he could stop it, and he saw the angry tightening of Jeanne's mouth. He hastily added, "It's too dangerous for a woman."

Quietly, Jeanne said, "There are two women out there right now with Matt Briggs and his men, and that's about as dangerous as you can get. And it's my fault."

"Briggs? You knew that outlaw?"

"I know who he is," Jeanne said. "And I know what he is."

Standing nearby, Forrest nodded. "So that's Matt Briggs. I thought he looked familiar. I saw him in Albuquerque." He smiled at Jeanne. "I'm afraid Mr. Davis is right, my dear. This is no business for a lady."

Jeanne took a deep breath to control the anger she felt at the patronizing tone in the gambler's voice. "That's where you're wrong, Mr. Forrest," she said. "It's very much my business." She turned to Stuart. "Are you going to give me a gun or not?"

Stuart studied her face, read the determination in her features, the flare of emotion in her eyes. Somehow, she looked different again, not at all like the plain, unassuming woman she had first appeared to be. Evidently there were a great many facets to Jeanne Townsend. And he could not help but wonder who she really was.

"Let's see what you can do with one," he said abruptly.

He took an Adams revolver out of the bin and stuck it out toward her, butt first. She took it, her small hand closing around the grips and holding the heavy weapon with no sign of strain. He dug out a box of .45 cartridges from the bin and flipped it to her; with her free hand, she deftly caught it.

As he watched her loading the gun, his eyes narrowed with interest. She seemed to know what she was doing, all right. Forrest was watching her with equal intensity, as were the others in the room.

"I really don't think this is a good idea," Forrest said. "It would be better if you stayed here at the station."

Kimbrough spoke up. "I agree. This is going to be dangerous enough without us having to spend our time watching out for a woman."

The look Jeanne gave him was hard and cold. "We're wasting time," she snapped. "If I have to prove myself to all of you, let's get on with it." She turned and strode toward the door.

Forrest and Kimbrough looked at Stuart, who shrugged and followed Jeanne.

She paused just outside the door, looking around for a suitable target. Pausing behind her, Stuart said, "You can't shoot out here. There's not enough light."

The moon had risen by now, its circle nearly full, and it cast a silvery glow down over the clearing. "It's bright enough," Jeanne said. She pointed. "See the branch hanging down on that pine?"

Stuart looked in the direction she was indicating and saw the branch. The tree was a good thirty yards away. There was little chance she could hit it at that range, even in daylight. "I see it," he told her.

The gun in her hand tipped up. She grasped her right wrist with her left hand for extra support, and a second later the gun blasted. Stuart blinked his eyes against the muzzle flash, then looked for the low-hanging branch on the pine tree. It was gone.

Stuart frowned, and Jeanne glanced over her shoulder at him and said, "Not enough?"

The gun roared twice more, and two more branches went spinning to the ground, clipped off the tree by the bullets. A whistle of admiration came from Stuart.

"Nice shooting," he said.

That was an understatement. It was damn good shooting, he knew—some of the best he had ever seen. And it added another mystery to this redheaded woman.

"Well, do I come along or not?" Jeanne demanded.

"You can shoot," Stuart admitted. "But I still can't agree to putting a woman in such danger."

Jeanne opened her mouth and was about to reply hotly something to the effect that it was Benjamin Kimbrough he should be worrying about and not her, but she thought better of it. Still, his arrogance was infuriating. It was becoming apparent that dealing with Stuart Davis was like running into a brick wall. But sometimes brick walls could be knocked down. . . .

Holding the gun down at her side, Jeanne started to stalk toward the doorway. Stuart could tell how upset she was, and he started to move aside to let her pass.

There was a sudden flicker of movement, a foot hooking behind his knee, a hand smacking into his chest and shoving, and before he knew what was happening, Stuart went down. He landed hard on the ground just outside the door, the breath puffing out of his lungs. Before he could even start to react, the cold metal of a gun barrel was snugged against his throat.

Jeanne grinned down at him wickedly from her position crouched above. "You ready to stop arguing?" she asked. "Because you really don't have much choice. Unless you put me under lock and key, there's nothing to stop me from going after Briggs and his men—whether you let me come along or not. And that's exactly what I'd do, so let's stop wasting time."

"Could be you're right," he said after a moment, a smile threatening to break out. "We are wasting time."

She took the gun away from his throat and straightened. Stuart climbed to his feet, feeling slightly embarrassed that she had taken him down so easily. Of course, he had not been expecting it. But that was no excuse. From what she had shown so far, she was good—damned good. She handled herself better than a lot of men he had known.

Stuart turned to the others, knowing that even after

what they had just seen, they would still be looking to him
for leadership. After all, he was an ex-lawman. An ex-
lawman who could not seem to put his past behind him, he
thought. First the four outlaws the night before, and now
this double kidnapping for God knew what reason.

Those thoughts kicked up some interesting ideas in
his head. Maybe somebody besides God did know why
tonight's events had taken place. Jeanne seemed to know
what was going on. She had known who Briggs was, and
she had implied that she was the one he was really looking
for. If that was the case, the two soiled doves had been
taken by mistake. Then there was the matter of the envelope she had slipped him at the station.

Stuart suddenly remembered that the four gunmen
who had ridden in the night before had been looking for a
redheaded woman who was probably heading north. Jeanne
fit that description, all right.

It was clear that he was going to have to have a long
talk with her sooner or later, Stuart decided. Sooner, if
possible.

"We'll get some horses saddled up," he said. "It's a
good thing those men didn't think to stampede the teams
in the corral." He looked up and down at Jeanne. "That's
not much of an outfit for traipsing in the woods."

Jeanne glanced down at the somber woolen dress.
"You're right," she admitted. She turned to George Davis,
who was the closest to her size among the men. "Do you
think you might have some pants and a shirt I could
borrow?"

"Reckon I could rustle somethin' up," George allowed. "But I can't promise how good it'll fit." He went
into the station to look for the clothes, and Jeanne followed.

Stuart jerked his head at Forrest and Kimbrough.
"Come on," he said. "We'll get the horses."

The horses in the corral were skittish as the three
men saddled them. Stuart pushed aside the bay gelding
he had ridden earlier in the day and picked out a sturdy-
looking buckskin for himself and his father's pinto for
Jeanne. The other horses were accustomed to pulling a
stagecoach, not to being used as saddle mounts, but they
settled down under Stuart's gentle hand.

"These saddles aren't the best," he told the other two men, gesturing at the spare saddles they were putting on two of the horses. Stuart and George each had their own saddle, and those were well cared for, while the other two were kept in a storage shed at the back of the station. "That's the best we can do," Stuart went on. "It'll be better than riding bareback."

George was coming from the front of the station carrying a couple of bedrolls and a sack of food when they led the horses around from the corral. He tied them down as Stuart asked, "Where's Jeanne?"

"In there changin'," George replied, leaning his head toward the building. "That there's sure an uncommon gal, son. I can't rightly figure her out."

"Neither can I," Stuart muttered. When he moved his arm, he felt the crackle of the envelope she had slipped to him. He had meant to look at it before now, but in the press of events had forgotten it. He reached inside his jacket to the small pocket where he had stuffed the envelope. He pulled it out and started to smooth it. In the glow coming through the door from the lanterns inside, he saw writing on the paper. Squinting, he made out the words: Pinkerton Detective Agency, Denver, Colorado.

"I'll take that back now, if you don't mind," Jeanne said quietly.

Stuart had not heard her come out of the station. He glanced at her and then looked again in surprise.

She was wearing an old pair of denims and a blue-and-white checked shirt. The pants were rolled up at the cuff and cinched in at the waist with a piece of rope. The sleeves of the shirt were rolled up, as well.

Stuart had seen those clothes many times before, in fact the shirt was George's best, but they never looked the way they did now. And Jeanne looked considerably different, too. Her red hair was no longer mousy but instead fell in loose waves to her shoulders. The light coming from inside struck glowing highlights off it. She had a look of freedom, almost wildness, about her now. The transformation from her previous prim appearance was remarkable.

Stuart became aware that she was holding her hand out toward him and realized that she was waiting for him to return the envelope. He gave it to her and watched her tuck it into the bosom of the shirt. She seemed to be waiting for him to ask her about it, but he decided not to for the time being. First he wanted some time to think about everything that had happened. Then Jeanne Townsend was going to have to come up with some answers.

Stuart mounted up, and the other three followed suit. Jeanne and Forrest seemed to handle their horses fairly well, though it was obvious that neither of them were used to riding much. Kimbrough was downright awkward, but he managed as best he could.

"We'll be back as soon as we can," Stuart said to George. "There'll be another northbound stage through tomorrow. You can send word into Taos by it, and I'm sure the sheriff there will send someone out to help."

"Don't you worry none about me, boy," George said testily. "I got Fred patched up, and he's sleepin' pretty quiet now. I'll keep an eye on him and the little gal. You just catch up to them bastards and give 'em what for."

Stuart grinned. "So long, Pa."

Kimbrough gave Marjorie a quick hug and instructed her to do whatever George told her. She buried her face against his shoulder and said in a low voice, "Please be careful, Papa."

"I will," Kimbrough said somewhat gruffly. He let her down and then turned his horse to follow the others out of the clearing.

George and Marjorie watched them go. It took only a minute for the shadowy forms to fade into the woods. Then George looked down at the teenager and said, "Reckon you can keep an eye on that young feller for me and let me know if he starts wakin' up?"

Marjorie thought about how handsome Fred Barker was and how helpless and vulnerable he had looked stretched out on the cot with his side heavily bandaged. "Why, I'd be glad to help you look after him, Mr. Davis," she said eagerly.

Chapter Ten

"**T**he trail leads north," Stuart told the others as they entered the woods. "Tracking by moonlight is going to be slow. But we can't get impatient or we'll lose the trail for sure."

Jeanne frowned in the darkness. North? Why was Briggs heading north with the women? She had assumed that he would go south, back to Albuquerque. Landreth would want to see the captives as soon as possible, that much was certain. Of course, Landreth was expecting Briggs to return with only one redhead, not two.

If Briggs was heading north, that meant Landreth had left Albuquerque and journeyed northward himself. If he was on a good horse, knew where he was going, and did not have to stick to the stage roads, he could have gotten ahead of them—he might even have made it to Taos by now if he had stopped and switched mounts along the way. If that was the case and Landreth had gone to Taos, he must have an important reason, Jeanne mused. And if her thinking was correct, Landreth would have told Briggs to bring her there when he had captured her.

Jeanne did not want to think about what might happen when Briggs showed up with Roseanne and Casey. Landreth would be furious, and he would take that anger out on Briggs, who would probably pass it on to the two women. There was a very good chance that both of them would wind up dead. If that happened, Jeanne thought, it would be her fault.

Riding beside Jeanne, Stuart looked at her face, grim

in the moonlight, and once again wondered who she was. She handled a gun like a professional, and no ordinary woman would have been able to put him down on the ground like that. There was also the business about the Pinkerton Detective Agency to ponder. This whole affair was complicated and perhaps bigger than anything he had ever encountered.

Curiosity was one reason he was out here riding a dangerous trail in the dark. He had made up his mind that he was through being a lawman, through with guns and killing. But regardless of whether he stuck to that decision, there were some things a man could not tolerate, and kidnapping helpless women was one of them. He knew he could not live with himself if he did not do something to try to help Roseanne and Casey. Besides, maybe this way he would find out just what Jeanne was up to. And whether he liked it or not, he had to admit that he was attracted to her—that he wanted to help her and protect her, as much as she would allow it. Not that she appeared to need much protection.

Lloyd Forrest was having similar thoughts. It had been years since he had done anything without thinking of the possible benefit to himself, but now he found himself riding along behind Stuart and Jeanne into something that might well get him killed. All because he had had an unexpected attack of chivalry. His family had originally been from the South, and he supposed a small part of him was ingrained with the Southern-gentleman attitude. He felt no special passion for either Roseanne or Casey; he had already sampled the charms of both and found them pleasant enough bedmates for an hour or two, but that was all there was to it. Still, he did not want to see either one of them hurt, and he was sure that was how their ordeal would end if no one helped them.

Benjamin Kimbrough's mind was even more unsettled. He had no real idea why he was out here bruising his behind on a horse and risking his life for two common sluts. The money he had lost could be replaced. Painful though its theft had been, it was not worth his life. This was what Marjorie wanted him to do, however, and he had always had an unreasonably soft spot in his heart for his youngest daughter. For some ridiculous reason, she thought of the whores as her friends, and Kimbrough knew he would be letting her down if he did not do whatever he could to help them. Still, he was not too concerned about letting her down in regard to the two women. What really worried him was the thought that she might not think him a man. *Well*, he thought unhappily, *Marjorie will see how wrong she is if I wind up dead.*

Kimbrough bit back a groan. He was already sore from riding—he had not even been on a horse for months until tonight—and the big Henry rifle, slung over his shoulder, was already getting heavy. He wished he were back in Albuquerque, safely in the bosom of his family.

Stuart followed the trail as best he could in the moonlight, moving slowly, sometimes stopping his horse for long moments while he studied the ground. Occasionally he had to dismount and kneel for a closer look to pick up the tracks of the men they were following. The trail continued to lead north.

The moon slid down the sky, growing more orange as its light faded. Finally, when they had been riding for several hours, Stuart reined in and said quietly, "We'd better stop now. The trail's going to be too hard to follow until we have more light."

"You mean we'll have to wait until morning?" Jeanne asked. The prospect of a delay chafed her.

"No more than a half hour or so," Stuart said. "It'll start getting light by then. Anyway, we can all use some rest, and so can the horses."

Jeanne could not argue with that. The events of the last two hectic days had begun to catch up with her. Riding in the wagon with the cowboys, then the long journey in the stagecoach, now the all-night ride . . . it was no wonder she was bone tired.

She slipped down out of the saddle and tied the reins to a nearby bush. They were on a hillside covered with thick grass, and the pines had thinned somewhat. To the west, the mountains rose high into the heavens, and even though they could not be seen in the darkness, their presence could almost be felt.

Kimbrough let out a low moan as he dismounted.

"Infernal beast!" he muttered under his breath as he tied the horse. He would not be able to walk right for a week, and he was firmly convinced he would not be able to sit down for a month.

Forrest felt a great deal of stiffness in his own muscles as he got down from his horse, but he did not say anything. He was not going to descend to the level of the merchant and waste his breath complaining. Instead, he found a fairly smooth spot underneath a pine and sat down, leaning his back against the trunk. The dirt was probably ruining his suit, but he was too tired to care. He reached inside his jacket and found a small silver flask. Uncapping it, he tilted the vessel to his lips and drank thirstily, the whiskey burning a path to his stomach.

Stuart frowned at the gambler. "You won't be any good to anybody if you're drunk," he said.

"I haven't been drunk in fifteen years, sir," Forrest said stiffly.

"And I'd like to see to it you live another fifteen," Stuart replied, his tone as taut as Forrest's. "There's no point in taking chances."

After a moment, Forrest shrugged and replaced the flask inside his jacket. The little group had plenty of common enemies without fighting each other.

Kimbrough had seen the gambler's flask and licked his lips. He was not ordinarily a drinking man, but a jolt of whiskey might be just the thing he needed now to brace him up. He had just started to walk over to the tree where Forrest was sitting when Stuart had spoken up and had convinced Forrest to put the liquor away.

Instead, Kimbrough asked Stuart, "Do you know if there's a stream near here where I can get a drink?"

Stuart took a canteen from his saddlebags. "I filled it at the station." He handed the canteen to Kimbrough. "Even in a country like this with lots of creeks and rivers, it's best to keep water handy."

Kimbrough drank eagerly for a moment, and when he paused, Stuart reached out and took the canteen from him. For a moment, Kimbrough seemed about to protest, but then he changed his mind.

Stuart carried the canteen over to where Jeanne was

standing beside her horse. "Here," he said, offering it to her. "And you'd better sit down and get some rest. We'll be riding pretty hard once the sun's up."

She took the canteen and drank gratefully; then she handed it back to Stuart and sank down cross-legged, putting her back against a tree trunk, as Forrest had.

Stuart glanced across the hillside at Kimbrough and the gambler. Both men were several yards away and did not seem to be paying any attention to them. He sat down near Jeanne and cuffed his hat onto the back of his head. "It's time we had a talk," he said. He could see her turn her head to look at him, but in the shadows, he could not read her expression.

"A talk about what?" she asked.

"About who you are. You're sure as hell not the schoolteacher I took you for at first," Stuart said bluntly.

Jeanne laughed softly. "You thought I was a schoolmarm?"

"That, or maybe a clerk in a store."

"And I don't look like that anymore."

"No, ma'am. You sure as hell don't." Stuart paused, afraid that he might have offended her, and then went on, "I don't mean there's anything wrong with the way you look now—"

"Thank you," Jeanne said dryly.

"What I meant," Stuart went on doggedly, "is that you're mixed up in all of this some way, and I want to know how. Those men were really after *you*, weren't they?"

Jeanne sighed. "I'm afraid they were."

"There's something you may not know. Four men rode into the station night before last. They were looking for a redheaded woman, too."

For a moment, Jeanne was silent. Then she asked, "What happened?"

"One of them recognized me as a lawman," Stuart said heavily. "They were on the dodge, and they went for their guns. They shouldn't have. Two of them are dead now."

"You had to shoot them?" she said.

"Yes. My father and I captured the other two, and I

turned them over to the sheriff in Santa Fe this morning."
He looked up at the night sky. The stars seemed a bit less
bright now. "Yesterday morning, I should say. And you
haven't answered my question."

"No, I haven't." Jeanne leaned her head against the
rough bark of the tree trunk, debating within herself just
how much she should tell Stuart Davis. He seemed to be
a good man, a solid man, and he was not short of courage.
But there was something about him that made her cautious.

"I'll tell you about it," she said, coming to a decision.
"But you've got to answer a question for me first."

Stuart frowned. It seemed to him that she was the
one who should be providing the answers. But if answering her question was the only way he was going to get the
full story . . .

"All right. What do you want to know?"

"Why have you decided to resign as a deputy marshal?"

He had halfway expected that question. She had to
have doubts about him, and she wanted those doubts
resolved before she put herself in his hands. Stuart could
not blame her for that. But the question and the memories
it aroused were still painful.

"I was wounded a few months ago," he said quietly.
"That's why I've been on a leave of absence from the
marshal's office, to let my arm heal up. It's recovered
about as much as it's going to."

"What about the rest of you?"

"I'd say the same thing's true of the rest of me. I've
recovered as well as I'm going to."

She would have to drag it out of him, Jeanne saw.
She hated doing that, hated the pain it was clearly causing
him. But if she was going to trust him, she had to know
more. "You were wounded in the line of duty?" she
prodded.

Stuart nodded. "Trying to catch some bandits who
had been holding up stagecoaches. We set a trap for them,
my partner and I. It didn't work out. My partner—hell,
he was my best friend, too—he was killed. If only I had
realized sooner that the outlaws had their own trap set
up."

Now that he was talking, the story began to spill out.

Jeanne listened in silence as he told her about the barricade across the road and the dummy with its threatening message. He did not try to make himself sound like any kind of hero as he told her about the long walk he had made for help after he was wounded.

Finally he was through, and Jeanne did not say anything for a long moment as she thought over what she had heard. Then, she said, "It sounds to me as if you did all you could. I don't think it was your fault."

"I know that, but maybe if my reactions had been quicker—if I had shouted sooner . . ."

"Were you in charge? Were you his boss?"

Stuart shook his head. "We were equal partners."

"Then he was responsible for taking care of himself."

He looked at her bleakly, able to see her better now that the sky was lightening. "He was my friend, and I keep wondering if somehow I let him down," he said simply.

Jeanne looked at him for a long moment and then said, "I get the feeling that it's not the past that's really troubling you, but the future."

Stuart cocked his head at her. "How do you mean?"

"You're worried that you may have lost your edge— the edge that allowed you to brace those four men in a Fort Worth saloon. You know you weren't responsible for your friend's death, but you're worried that you may cause someone else's in the future."

Rather than answer directly and admit aloud that she was right, Stuart looked away and replied, "A lawman almost has to have a blind faith in his abilities. I'm not so sure I have that anymore."

"Maybe the only thing you've lost is the rash confidence of youth—a recklessness that could just as easily get you in trouble as save you. You may just end up a better lawman because of what you've gone through."

"All I know is that I don't want to be responsible for getting anybody killed," Stuart went on after a moment. "That's why I'm not going back to the marshal's office."

"You're going to throw away your career?"

He shrugged and said, "Maybe I'll work on my own, do a little bounty hunting."

"You didn't hesitate when it came to going after Briggs and trying to rescue those women," Jeanne pointed out.

Stuart's face hardened. "That's different. Briggs came into my father's station and kidnapped those women. No man worth his salt would let him just get away with that. And *you* still haven't told me why it all happened and what your connection is with the Pinkertons."

Jeanne shot a glance at him. "You read the address on the envelope," she said, her tone faintly accusing.

"You gave it to me," Stuart shot back. "I figured you intended for me to get it to the Pinkertons if anything happened to you."

"That's exactly what I did intend. It contains very important evidence that needs to be turned over to them."

Stuart had suspected as much. He said, "I reckon you intended to hire them to straighten things out."

Jeanne smiled and tried not to laugh. "You thought I planned on hiring the Pinkertons?" she asked.

"Didn't you?"

Jeanne shook her head. "I'm afraid not, Stuart." She paused for effect and then said, "You see, I work for them myself."

Stuart just stared at her, feeling as if someone had smacked him in the face. He was shocked, but at the same time he realized that everything she had done so far supported her claim.

"You're a Pinkerton agent," he said after a moment, his voice flat, neither believing nor disbelieving.

"That's right. I'm afraid I don't have any sort of identification to show you, but when you're working under an assumed identity, that would defeat the purpose, wouldn't it?"

Stuart's mouth quirked in a grimace. "I suppose Jeanne Townsend isn't your real name, either."

"It just so happens that it is. I used the name Jeanne Fontanne in Albuquerque, but when I went on the run I thought it best to use my real name, in case the Pinkertons have to track me down."

Slowly, Stuart shook his head. "I'm afraid I'm not sure about any of this."

Jeanne leaned forward, evidently eager for him to

believe her. "Look, I told you I don't have any identification, but would it help if I showed you the papers I'm carrying? I'm not sure myself what it's all about, but I know something bad is going to happen if I don't stop it somehow."

Stuart held out his hand, and Jeanne reached inside her shirt and took out the envelope. She handed it over, but not before she had glanced over at Forrest and Kimbrough and saw that they were not paying any attention. She and Stuart had been talking in low-pitched voices so that the other two could not overhear, but neither of the two men seemed interested in anything except resting while they could. The long night of riding had taken a lot out of them.

Stuart opened the envelope and removed the papers, spreading them on his knee. The dawn light was still dim, the sun not yet having topped the eastern horizon, and he had to squint to make out the words. After a moment of reading, he glanced up at Jeanne, a frown furrowing his forehead. "I've heard of this fella," he said, pointing at the signature on the notes. "Wasn't he part of what they called the Santa Fe Ring?"

Jeanne nodded. "That's right. Lew Wallace pretty well broke up the ring when be became governor of the territory, but most of the men involved still have some power and influence. This man appears to be hatching some kind of scheme with Darryl Landreth."

"And I've heard Landreth's name," Stuart mused.

"You should have, being a deputy marshal. He's the biggest crook in New Mexico. He owns a saloon in Albuquerque called the Black Bull, and Briggs works for him. They're part of just about everything illegal that goes on in this part of the country."

"Sounds as if you know quite a bit about him."

"I was sent down here to get the goods on him," Jeanne said grimly. "The agency was hired by the family of a man Landreth killed back east. He had already beaten that charge, but the family was hoping we could turn up the evidence that would bring Landreth to justice for some of his other crimes."

Stuart had been watching her face and listening to

her voice as she talked, and he had not been able to detect anything except sincerity. He said, "Seems like a mighty big job for a woman, especially one by herself."

Jeanne flushed slightly, and Stuart knew he had hit a nerve. "Being a woman made it possible for me to get a job in Landreth's saloon," she said, "and that's how I was able to get those papers."

"Used your feminine wiles on him, eh?" Stuart knew he was being rude, but if he was to understand what was happening, he had to know all of the truth.

"I know what you're implying," Jeanne said coolly. "Things didn't get that far . . . but don't think I wouldn't have been able to handle the situation if they had." She paused and then added tartly, "It's attitudes like yours that make me want to work without a partner. Men never think I'm capable of getting somewhere with guts and brains."

"I didn't say that," Stuart said quietly. "You seem to have plenty of both. But there's no point in denying that you're a beautiful woman."

"And you're a brave man, but that doesn't stop you from wallowing in self-doubts because of what happened to your friend."

Jeanne knew as soon as the words were out of her mouth that she had gone too far. She saw Stuart stiffen and felt ashamed that she had spoken so bluntly. But he had gotten under her skin with his comments, and he could not blame her for letting her emotions get the better of her. There was no time to worry about it now, however. The hurt feelings on both sides could be sorted out later. Assuming there was a later, that is.

Stuart took a deep breath. He had come to the same conclusion. They all had more important things to concern themselves with right now, like catching up to Briggs. It was light enough to be riding again now, but something in the notes had caught his eye. Using it as an opportunity to ease the tension, he held the papers closer so that Jeanne could see what he was pointing to and said, "Look at this. There's mention of a ranch in this letter, and over here it talks about a nearby pueblo. That mean anything to you?"

Jeanne shook her head. "I saw those references, but

they were so vague. There are a lot of ranches and pueblos in the territory."

"Reckon so, but Rancho de Taos is an earlier name for the town of Taos, and Taos Pueblo is the Indian settlement nearby. Seems to me like the notes could be referring to Taos and saying that that's where whatever they've got planned is going to happen."

Jeanne felt her pulse quicken. Stuart might have hit on something with his knowledge of the area and its history. His theory made sense, and even though they still did not know what Landreth was up to, knowing the location could be a big help.

"Briggs is still heading north," she said. "That's toward Taos, right?"

Stuart nodded.

"I figured Landreth must have gone north for some reason. Otherwise Briggs would be bringing the women south to Albuquerque. I think you may have figured out why. Whatever this plan is, it must be about to come to a head."

"Sounds like it to me." Stuart stood and looked down at her, reading the excitement in her features. He was ready now to accept her story about being a Pinkerton agent, and he held out a hand to help her up. "We'd better be riding," he said, lifting her to her feet.

Jeanne let her hand remain in Stuart's for a second longer than she had to. Their eyes met for a moment, and then she turned away, nodding.

"Yes," she said. "I think we've got an appointment in Taos."

Several yards away, Lloyd Forrest watched Stuart and Jeanne looking at the papers and talking together in low voices. Forrest supposed he should have been more interested, but just now his mind was on other things.

He slipped a hand inside his jacket and brought out the folded piece of paper he had been studying in Santa Fe. Ever since the letter from his brother had found him in Albuquerque, he had been rereading it at quiet, reflective moments like this one. Jeanne and Stuart might have their secrets, judging by the way they were poring over the papers she had taken from inside her shirt, but in a

way so did he. He knew that Jeanne had thought he was
not watching when she had removed the envelope, but he
had seen her quick movement. The truth of the matter
was that he did not particularly care what had brought this
business about. He just wanted to get on with rescuing
Roseanne and Casey and then travel on to his destination.

Forrest looked at the letter for a long moment in the
misty dawn light and then slid it into its hiding place in his
jacket. He had a great deal of thinking to do.

Chapter Eleven

Matt Briggs reined in his horse as the sun began to peek over the summits of the mountains to the east. He breathed deeply of the cool air and then let his shoulders slump as weariness overtook him. He felt as though he had been in the saddle forever.

"Five minutes," he called to his men. "That's all."

Some of them began to grumble. They were as tired as he was, but as far as Briggs was concerned, that still did not give them the right to complain.

"We'll take a longer break later in the morning," he told the men. "Until then, keep your traps shut!"

They heeded the cold warning in his voice and dismounted, getting down to stretch their legs and give a short rest to their exhausted horses.

The two women were hauled down from the saddles. They had long since given up on their sobbing and wailing, realizing that Briggs was not going to be swayed by emotional displays or claims of innocence. Now both women were dry-eyed, their faces drawn into gaunt lines by strain. They stood, head down, legs trembling slightly from exhaustion.

Briggs walked over to them and reached out to cup Casey's chin. He jerked her head back so that he could grin at her. "You ladies look tired," he jeered. "Guess you're used to lying down on the job."

"You've got us wrong, mister," Roseanne said, making one last try to convince him. "Neither one of us is the woman you're looking for, I promise you. We been together for years. We were together in Albuquerque. I swear we never did anything bad."

"What do you call whoring?" Briggs asked.

"A job," Casey said harshly. "We never hurt nobody, I swear it."

"You're wasting your time lying for each other."

Casey's face contorted in fury. "Then go to hell, you son of a bitch! I'd like to get my hands loose and on a knife. I'd show you a few things—"

Briggs slapped her face, jerking her head to the side and rocking her back on her heels. As he pointed a shaking finger at her, he snapped, "You just keep a civil tongue in your head, slut! I got to deliver you alive, but nothing was said about unmarked!"

He turned and stalked away, leaving the two women to lean on each other, seeking what scant comfort they could in their mutual fear.

Briggs gestured to two of his men. "Could be somebody coming up on our back trail," he told them, and for the first time he wondered if perhaps he should have killed everyone at the way station. Shaking off the doubts, he continued, "Telford, I want you and Rains to split off here and wait to see if anyone's trailing us. If they are, you know what to do."

A vicious grin split Telford's face. "You bet, boss. We'll handle 'em."

Briggs nodded. There were not any more hardened men in his outfit than Telford and Rains . . . except himself. They would put a stop to any pursuit.

"The rest of you mount up," Briggs called. "Get those women on the horses. Come on! Time's a-wasting!"

With the sun up, Stuart was able to track the outlaws much more easily, and he and his companions were making better time. Before they had started back on the trail, they had eaten quickly from the sack George had prepared. At least it kept down the complaints of hunger.

Jeanne's experience in the wilderness was limited, but it seemed to her that the tracks they were following were getting fresher. That meant they were cutting into

Briggs's lead. With any luck, they would catch up to him before the day was over.

As Stuart had expected, Kimbrough had complained when it was time to start again, but Forrest had said little. The gambler seemed to keep to himself most of the time. He was a strange man, Stuart thought. But that was true of about ninety percent of the people on the frontier, he knew. There was something, some indefinable quality, that set them off from average citizens, and sometimes the paths they went down were determined by nothing but luck.

Pushing those thoughts out of his head, Stuart concentrated on following the tracks of the horses up ahead. Soon his mount topped a ridge and started down the slope on the other side. The trail led across a little ravine and then turned up a steeper, boulder-littered ridge on the other side. Stuart lifted his eyes from the tracks and glanced at the slope across the ravine, at first seeing nothing out of the ordinary . . . except a pebble, bouncing down from a clump of rocks about midway up the ridge.

"Look out!" Stuart yelled, leaving the saddle in a dive that landed him heavily and painfully on the ground. He heard the blast of a shot and the whine of a bullet passing close by his head.

Jeanne jerked up on the reins, pulling her horse into a tight turn as she looked for the source of the shot. Another rifle shot cracked as she pulled the Adams from the waistband of her pants. She saw a puff of smoke from the opposite ridge and squeezed off a shot toward it, the Adams bucking against her palm.

Stuart had his gun out now and was firing toward the ambushers. There were at least two of them, he could tell, and both were firing rifles. Stuart was lying in the open—a damned bad place to be. After he had fired off three rounds, he rolled to the side, putting himself behind a small slab of rock. It was not much cover, but it would have to do.

There was not much cover on this whole side of the ravine, in fact, other than a few scrubby trees and some small rocks like the one Stuart was crouching behind. Jeanne left the saddle and landed on her feet, staggering a few steps as she caught her balance on the slope. Two more steps put her behind one of the trees.

Benjamin Kimbrough was not given to cursing, but he yelled a heartfelt "Dammit!" as he dropped out of his saddle and scurried to shelter. His horse immediately followed Stuart's and Jeanne's down along the ravine and away from the gunshots.

For a moment Kimbrough considered trying to make it back to the top of the ridge. He would be safe enough on the other side. But he knew he would be cut down before he could make half the distance, so he settled for flopping on his stomach in a most undignified manner and trying to make himself invisible behind a small outcropping of stone. He poked the barrel of his rifle past the rocks and triggered a shot, not really aiming, in the general direction of the opposite slope.

Moving smoothly, Lloyd Forrest dismounted and crouched behind one of the trees, about ten yards from Jeanne's position. He heard the flat *whap* of a slug passing inches from his ear. Calmly, he raised his pistol and began firing.

A bullet plucked at the crown of Stuart's black Stetson and spun the hat off his head. He grimaced, ducking down and thumbing fresh cartridges into his gun. He had the two men located now, right where he had suspected, in a group of boulders. That knowledge was not going to do him a whole hell of a lot of good, however, pinned down as he was. As all of them were. Two men with rifles could keep them bottled up here all day, and that thought put a bitter taste in Stuart's mouth. In all likelihood, Briggs and his two captives were getting farther away with each passing minute. And there was not a damn thing to be done about it.

The sun rose in the sky, heating the air in the ravine. Gunshots continued to echo until Stuart thought he was going to go deaf. So far, no one had been hit. He could see Jeanne and Forrest and Kimbrough firing ineffectually toward the gunmen, who were hidden behind plenty of cover on the other side of the ridge. The men could poke their rifles through little openings in the cluster of boulders and blaze away with impunity.

There had to be a way, Stuart told himself as he gazed up the slope behind the ambushers. He remembered the rolling pebble that had warned him, accidentally dislodged by a boot to go bounding down the incline. That pebble had knocked several others loose, creating a miniature landslide, raising tendrils of dust that had been blown away by the hot breeze. If he could just start another rock rolling, Stuart thought—a rock up the slope behind the would-be killers. There was just one problem with that idea, he saw, his heart sinking. There were not any big rocks where he needed them.

Well, he thought, his resolve stiffening, maybe a bunch of little rocks would do. The main thing he wanted was a diversion, a chance to work his way to one side so that he would have a better angle on the two men.

He tipped the barrel of the Colt up and started firing. The bullets kicked up dust as they thudded into the slope a good twenty feet above the ambushers.

Jeanne narrowed her eyes as she saw what Stuart was doing. At first she had thought he was just missing badly, but she knew that was unlikely. She saw fist-sized chunks of rock leap into the air when his bullets hit them, only to fall back and start rolling down toward the boulders.

A smile played over her lips. She raised her gun and began directing her bullets into the same area.

The trickle of rocks became a steady stream, kicking up a thick haze of dust. As he paused to reload, Stuart heard one of the outlaws across the way yell, "What the hell?" Both of them began to cough from the dust that was already drifting down to them.

Stuart glanced at Jeanne, met her eyes for a moment, and nodded in gratitude that she had understood what he was doing. Then he surged to his feet, running as fast as he could across the slope, bounding through the ravine and angling up the other side.

Suddenly bullets began to hum around him, and the dust in his nostrils smelled like fear. He pushed the fear away and went down on one knee to steady himself as he spotted the two members of Briggs's gang. From this angle, he had a clear shot at them as they crouched behind the boulders. He threw the Colt up and fired, letting the old instincts do their work.

One of the men suddenly dropped his rifle and clutched his chest, falling forward and rolling out from behind the boulders. Stuart saw more bullets smack into him, these shots coming from Jeanne and Forrest, but from the way the man had fallen, he was already dead.

The other one came out of his crouch, levering his Winchester and sending a hail of slugs toward Stuart. He took one step, carelessly exposing himself, and abruptly flung up his hands as blood spurted from his bullet-torn throat. He sprawled out on the slope next to his companion.

Jeanne looked over at Lloyd Forrest. She knew he had been the one to down the second gunman; she had been in the process of reloading when Stuart's maneuver had drawn him out into the open. The gambler's face was expressionless as he stepped out from behind the tree he had been using as cover.

"Hold your fire, Mr. Kimbrough!" Jeanne called to the businessman, who was still pumping shots wildly into the air. Most of his bullets were not hitting anything, but there was no point in taking unnecessary chances.

Stuart got to his feet as Jeanne, Forrest, and Kimbrough emerged from their shelter. Holding his Colt ready, he walked slowly toward the fallen gunmen. Both of them were dead, he saw, but he shoved them over onto their backs with a booted foot to make sure.

The other three came across the ravine and walked up the slope. Kimbrough paled and turned away when he saw the bloody corpses, but Stuart noted that Jeanne and Forrest seemed to be in full control of themselves. Jeanne studied the dead men and then said, "They were with Briggs last night at the station." Stuart and Forrest nodded.

Kimbrough turned back to them, but his eyes steadfastly avoided the bodies. He passed a hand over his sweating face and said, "I think we should turn back. We're just going to get those young women killed if we go on. That man Briggs is a butcher!"

"Yes, he is," Jeanne agreed coldly. "That's why we can't leave Roseanne and Casey in his hands."

"I concur," Forrest added. "This is just an example of how ruthless the man is. We have to go on."

Stuart did not waste any breath joining in the discussion. There was no question in his mind about whether or not to continue. Instead, he turned and walked up to the top of the ridge above where the ambushers had been hiding. He found what he had expected to find there.

"Their horses are tied up in the woods on the other side of the rise," he said when he rejoined the grim little group. "We should probably take them with us."

Jeanne nodded. "That way Roseanne and Casey won't have to double up with any of us later." She realized she was assuming they would be successful in their rescue attempt, but there was no point in expecting the worst.

"I'll go round up our horses," Stuart went on. The animals had fled down the ravine during the gun battle, but all four of them were still in sight. Stuart had started toward them when Jeanne reached out and put a hand on his arm, stopping him.

"We'll have two extra horses now," she said, looking thoughtful, "the horses belonging to these two men." She waved a hand at the corpses.

"That's right," Stuart said. His eyes narrowed. "You look like you've got an idea."

"I do, and it's simple," Jeanne explained, talking quickly because she knew Stuart would probably protest when he heard her plan. She gestured at the two dead men. "You and I change clothes with these two and take their horses. Briggs has to have stopped somewhere up ahead to rest. We catch up and ride in, and he doesn't realize who we really are until we're right there among them."

Stuart started shaking his head, but Jeanne ignored him and forged on with her plan.

"Forrest and Kimbrough follow behind us with the two spare horses and give us cover if we need it when we make our move. We grab Roseanne and Casey and get out of there."

Stuart's face was set in determined lines. "It might work," he said, "but not with you taking the part of one of the outlaws. That's too dangerous."

"I believe Stuart is right," Forrest spoke up. "I'm willing to accompany him in the masquerade, though."

Jeanne shook her head angrily. "I thought we had this argument back at the station," she snapped at Stuart. "Have you forgotten already about my little demonstrations?"

Stuart flushed slightly, getting angry now himself. "You're a good shot," he admitted. "But you took me by surprise when you threw me down."

"That's what we're going to do to Briggs, take him by surprise. Anyway," she went on, her jaw setting stubbornly, "it's my responsibility."

Stuart knew that she was talking about her job as a Pinkerton agent. The other two men were not aware of that fact, and he sensed that Jeanne wanted to keep it that way. He stared at her for a long moment, seeing the flare of emotion in her eyes. Then he said flatly, "It was your idea. I suppose you deserve a chance to make it work."

Jeanne grinned. "It'll work. You'll see."

Stuart turned his head to hide the concern that tugged at his features. He hoped she was right. It had taken more of an effort than he had expected to give in to her wishes. There was a surprisingly large part of him that was starting to feel downright protective of her, and he did not want to think about what that might mean.

"I still believe we should turn back," Kimbrough said. "We're going to wind up getting ourselves and those two women killed."

"Not if you do what I tell you to do," Jeanne said, her voice taking on a tone of command that made Kimbrough frown. She was tired of the businessman's whining and complaining. He had not been much good in this fight, but if he would keep his head and listen, he and Forrest could provide some very valuable assistance when it came time for the actual rescue attempt.

"If we're going to do this, we'd better get busy," Stuart said. "Briggs has slowed us down enough already."

He bent to the task of stripping the vests and jackets from the two dead outlaws. The shirts were bloody from the bullet wounds, and wearing them might give the masquerade away too early; also, there was no need to change pants, since they all were wearing denims.

When Jeanne had the man's outer clothing on, she buckled on the gun belt that the outlaw had worn and tucked her hair up under his battered black hat. The clothes were a little large on her, just as the other man's were a bit small on Stuart. He had to admit, though, that anyone looking at them from a distance probably would take them for the two outlaws, especially since they would be riding the dead men's horses.

Forrest had led the animals from the other side of the ridge. Stuart put his own Winchester in one of the saddle boots while Jeanne appropriated a rifle from one of the kidnappers.

"We'll be pushing on pretty fast," Stuart told Forrest and Kimbrough as he swung up into the saddle. "You won't be able to move as fast leading two horses. Reckon you can follow our trail?"

"Don't worry," Forrest assured him. "I'm more at home in a saloon, as I'm sure you've gathered, but I can read signs well enough to stay on your trail."

Jeanne mounted up. The horse was nervous and jumped around for a second, probably made anxious by a strange rider. Jeanne kept a tight rein on him and calmed him down, leaning forward over his neck as she patted him and talked to him in a soothing voice.

She glanced up at Stuart. "I'm ready to go whenever you are," she said.

"Let's ride," he replied, and they spurred the horses up the slope and over the top of the ridge, and a moment later they were gone from sight.

Men and animals could be pushed only so hard, Matt Briggs realized. Late in the morning, as they rode into a peaceful meadow, he saw how his companions were lagging, and he felt the same weariness. "All right, hold up," he called to them, sliding from the saddle. "We'll rest awhile."

Gratefully, the other five outlaws dismounted. Two of the men started a small fire to heat some coffee, while another passed around some jerky.

Briggs walked over to Roseanne and Casey, both of whom were glaring at him with hate in their eyes. He grinned and said, "If I cut you loose, you won't run, will you?"

"I wouldn't count on that," Casey spat at him.

"I'd hate to have to shoot you," he said, still grinning, his eyes like ice. "Still, a slug in the knee wouldn't kill you. You'd live to get where we're going. You'd just never be able to walk right again."

"You'd do that, too, wouldn't you?" Roseanne asked in a voice barely above a whisper.

"Damn right I would, lady. What about it? Do I have your word you won't try to get away?"

Roseanne said bitterly, "What good is the word of a whore?"

"Good enough for me." Briggs slid his pistol out of its holster. "As long as I've got this."

"We won't try to get away," Casey said dully, her spirit waning. "Could we have something to eat and some of that coffee?"

"I think that can be arranged."

Briggs slid his knife out of its sheath and cut the cords binding their hands. Both of the women flinched as the cold steel touched their skin, but Briggs's hand was steady. The blade cut only the ropes and did not nick the skin underneath.

As Roseanne and Casey massaged their wrists, Briggs said, "You might say thank you."

"And I might say go to hell," Casey responded, a little of her natural fire returning.

Briggs's hand shot out, his fingers catching her under the chin and roughly tilting her head back. He jerked her closer to him and reached up with his other hand to fondle her breast. Casey stiffened and stared at him with a mixture of fear and rage in her eyes, but she kept silent.

"You still don't understand, do you?" Briggs hissed. "I've got your life right in my hands. You could make things a lot more pleasant for all of us."

Roseanne leaned forward, knowing that Briggs's grip on Casey's face had to be painful. "We'll do whatever you want," she said hurriedly. "Just don't hurt us, all right?"

Briggs released Casey with a little shove. "I don't want anything from you sluts." He laughed harshly. "I was just seeing if you'd run true to form. You did."

He turned on his heel and stalked away, the crazy anger slowly dying in his eyes.

As soon as he was gone, Roseanne and Casey found a place to sit, wincing as they did so; neither was used to riding a horse. One of the kidnappers brought them jerky and coffee, which they accepted expressionlessly. In a soft voice, the man said, "Briggs told us to leave you alone for the time bein', but it ain't always goin' to be that way." His beard-stubbled face split in a lecherous grin. "I'm lookin' forward to that."

Neither woman looked up at him, and after they had ignored him for a moment, he shrugged and went away. Casey tore off a hunk of the jerky with her teeth, chewed it for a few seconds, and then said around it, "They're all crazy. They had no call to do this."

"They thought one of us was somebody else," Roseanne said. "And they're too stupid and stubborn to change their minds." Her voice broke slightly as she went on, "What do you think is going to happen to us?"

"Hell, when they get to wherever they're taking us, their boss will realize there's been a mistake. He'll probably just send us on our way."

"You really think that's what'll happen?"

Casey smiled thinly. "I don't know, honey. I just don't know. All I'm sure of is that I'd like to be alone with that Briggs fella for about ten minutes. I'd give him a time he'd never forget."

"You would?"

"I figure it'd take him about that long to bleed to death."

Roseanne smiled along with Casey. It was a pleasant thought, all right. Both of them had lived difficult lives and seen plenty of violence, but they had never been in a situation where they were so helpless.

"Maybe somebody from that stage station will come after us," Roseanne said.

"Like Lloyd Forrest?" Casey laughed humorlessly. "He didn't seem too interested in us anymore. I think he actually had eyes for that prissy little gal in the black dress."

"You're right," Roseanne said. "But maybe that young man who worked at the station—"

"The one who used to be a marshal?" Casey nodded thoughtfully. "He did seem like the sort not to stand by and do nothing. God, I hope *somebody* comes after us."

"I think I'd kill myself before I let Briggs have his way with me," Roseanne said softly. "I know that sounds strange coming from a . . . a woman like me, but he just makes my skin crawl."

Casey shook her head. "Not me. I don't give a damn what he or any of the others do. I'm going to stay alive." She paused and then said, "I've got a score to settle with that bastard."

Across the meadow, Briggs had sat down by himself and was looking out across the grassy expanse, surrounded by pines and cedars. Wildflowers were blooming, and the sky overhead was clear and blue. Mountains hulked in the distance to both the west and east, the Rockies in the west looming higher and more majestic. It was a beautiful spot to anyone who stopped in the right frame of mind to appreciate its splendors. But to Matt Briggs, it was just one step closer to Landreth and the payoff for returning the woman he was seeking—a payoff that already had jumped from fifty to five hundred dollars before Briggs had left Albuquerque. But that was only the appetizer, for when that was done, there was an even more lucrative job to accomplish for Landreth.

As he chewed a piece of jerky and swallowed some of the strong coffee his men had brewed, Briggs thought about that job—a job that not only would make him a rich man but would bring the government of New Mexico Territory to its knees. For soon after Briggs and his men arrived in Taos, Governor Lew Wallace would be a dead man.

Briggs had been riding his men so hard because he knew that he had to be in Taos by late that afternoon. Had he not found the redheaded woman in time, he would have abandoned the pursuit—his other job was that important. It was so important that even his men had no idea what was going to happen when they reached Taos. By the end of the day, however, everyone would know. And the territory of New Mexico would never be the same again.

Chapter Twelve

As Stuart and Jeanne followed the trail left by Matt Briggs and his men, Stuart did some quick mathematics. There had been eight outlaws at the way station. With two now dead, that left Briggs plus five others—unless more had joined up with him, something that was all too possible, Stuart knew.

He and Jeanne kept the horses at a fast trot. The country was still rocky and rugged, preventing them from traveling as quickly as he would have liked. Yet he was confident that sooner or later they would catch up to their quarry.

As the sun crept higher in the sky and the day grew hotter, the two of them rode through broad valleys lined with thick grass. It was beautiful country, Jeanne thought, wishing that she was in more of a mood to appreciate it. She allowed her thoughts to stray for a moment, and in her mind she was riding across this land with Stuart Davis at her side, only they were no longer bound on a desperate mission that would probably end with flaming guns. Their only mission involved each other. . . .

Jeanne tightened her jaw and gave a short, almost unnoticeable shake of her head. It was a nice dream, but for now that was all it was. First she had to deal with Matt Briggs, and beyond him, Darryl Landreth himself.

They had been riding for a little over an hour when Stuart suddenly reined in and called softly to Jeanne, "Hold it."

She pulled her horse to a stop beside his, and he lifted an arm to the north. "Somebody's got a fire going over there," he said.

Jeanne looked in the direction he was pointing and had to concentrate for several moments before she was able to spot the thin, almost colorless tendril of smoke. She had a feeling she never would have seen it without Stuart to point it out.

"Do you think it's Briggs?" she asked.

"Good chance of it," Stuart replied. "He and his men have to be tired. God knows we are, and they've been in the saddle even longer. And their horses should be next to foundering; they'll have to be rested."

"That's what I'm counting on," Jeanne said grimly.

"We'll take it a little slower from here on," Stuart told her. "We don't want to come up on them too quickly."

He kept his eyes on the smoke as they rode. Fifteen minutes later, when they reached the base of a hill, he held up a hand to signal another stop. Both of them swung down, and Stuart said in a soft voice, "They're probably just on the other side of that rise. We'd best leave the horses here and take a look on foot."

Jeanne nodded, saying nothing. There was no point in discussion until they made sure they had tracked down their quarry.

They started up the hill after hitching the horses to some brush. Stuart discovered that he could still move quietly when he had to, and Jeanne showed a surprising ability in that area. They cat-footed their way to the top of the hill, removed their borrowed hats, and carefully risked a glance over the crest of the ridge.

The gentle slope on the other side led down into one of the broad, shallow valleys, and in a clearing in the center of it were Matt Briggs, his remaining five men, and the two women.

Stuart felt a hand on his arm and looked over at Jeanne. Her grip was tight, matching the intensity on her face. She mouthed the words, *It's them*. Stuart nodded silently and jerked his head back the way they had come. He made his way down the hill, Jeanne following closely behind.

When she and Stuart had reached their horses, she said, "Did it look to you like Roseanne and Casey are all right?"

"Didn't look like they've been hurt. Of course, they were a good ways off."

"I suppose that now we wait for Forrest and Kimbrough to catch up."

Stuart nodded. "And let's hope it doesn't take them too long to get here. It doesn't look like Briggs is in any hurry to pull out, but you can never tell."

Stuart took the canteen from his saddle and offered it to Jeanne. She uncapped it and tilted it to her mouth, holding it there only a second before jerking it away and spitting out the mouthful of liquid. "That's not water!" she exclaimed.

Stuart frowned and reached out to take the canteen. He sniffed it, wrinkling his nose as the raw odor of whiskey burned into his nostrils. "It's not my canteen," he explained. "It was on the saddle, so I guess it belonged to one of those jaspers who ambushed us. I shook it when I mounted up to make sure it wasn't empty, but I didn't think to check what was in it."

Jeanne stepped over to her mount. There was a canteen on that saddle, as well, and when she uncapped it, the contents proved to be water. "Kind of stale," she said after sampling it and then offering it to Stuart. "It beats the stuff in that other one, though."

Stuart took a drink and then handed the canteen back to her and said, "We'd best get back up to the top of the slope and keep an eye on Briggs."

At the top of the hill, they settled down behind a clump of brush to wait for Forrest and Kimbrough. Stuart let his eyes rove over the clearing in the center of the valley, marking the locations of Briggs and his men. The women were sitting underneath a tree on the west side of the clearing. Briggs was seated on the ground near them, apparently making an occasional comment to them, though Roseanne and Casey seemed to be trying to ignore him. One of the men was crouched beside the small fire, and two more appeared to be asleep under a tree on the east side of the clearing. That left two men to watch the horses and wander along the perimeter of the crude little camp, rifles cradled in their arms.

"Still think your plan will work?" Stuart asked Jeanne in a whisper.

She nodded. "I'm sure of it. They're not expecting any trouble. You can tell that by looking at them."

She was probably right, Stuart thought. With the arrogant confidence of most outlaws, Briggs expected the men he had left behind to polish off anyone foolish enough to chase them. If they could turn Briggs's excess of confidence to their advantage—and if they were lucky—they might be able to rescue the two women without any bloodshed.

There was nothing for them to do now but wait, and after a few minutes the silence began to gnaw at Stuart's nerves. He looked over at Jeanne, who was still intently watching the outlaws. After a moment, she glanced at him and frowned. "What is it?" she asked.

"Just wondering how a woman like you wound up a Pinkerton agent," Stuart said, his voice still pitched low enough that the words would not carry down the hill into the valley.

A smile tugged at Jeanne's lips. "I've been asked that before. Usually the men who asked didn't really want to know. They were just making conversation."

"I want to know," Stuart said simply.

"I know you do." Jeanne thought for a moment and then went on, "I suppose it started with my father. He and Allan Pinkerton were policemen together, and when Mr. Pinkerton started his agency my father was one of his operatives." Again she hesitated, and Stuart saw a flicker of pain in her eyes. He began to wish he had not asked about her background.

Jeanne swallowed and continued, "He was killed on a job for the agency. Mr. Pinkerton is quite the thrifty Scot, as you may have heard, but he was more than generous in his offers to take care of my mother and my sisters and myself. But I was the oldest of the children, and I felt that I ought to pitch in and do something to help support the family."

"Reckon I can guess what you decided to do," Stuart put in.

Jeanne smiled again. "Mr. Pinkerton was certainly shocked when I told him I wanted to go to work for his agency. He refused point-blank . . . for about six months. By that time, I had worn him down enough to give me a chance."

Stuart imagined that Jeanne could be pretty persuasive. After all, she had talked him into letting her come along in the first place, and then she had convinced him to let her masquerade as one of the dead outlaws.

"Mr. Pinkerton started out trying to give me just the easy jobs, but I didn't like that. I wanted to be a full-fledged agent and take the jobs I was best suited for. When I proved I could handle everything he threw my way, he finally came around to my way of thinking. But then he started insisting that I work with a partner."

"And you didn't like that," Stuart said.

Jeanne grimaced. "I was good at what I was doing, Stuart. Damned good, if I do say so myself. I tried it his way, but I just seemed to work better alone. I didn't like having to depend on someone else."

"That can get you in trouble, all right," he said.

The tone of his voice told Jeanne that he was thinking about his own former partner, the deputy who had been killed in the stage holdup. She hesitated, not sure if she should say anything about it or not, but then she decided to plunge ahead. She liked Stuart Davis, and she did not like seeing him brood about the past.

"From what you've told me, it wasn't really your fault," she said. "It was just something that happened."

"I know, but that doesn't help Corey any."

Jeanne's eyes met his, and she said, "Listen, Stuart. I may not have been a deputy marshal, but our lines of work aren't that much different. And it's my professional opinion that you're a good lawman. I've seen how you handle yourself, how you got us out of that ambush back there. Nobody could have done it any better."

Stuart looked down, not saying anything. Maybe she was right. He just did not know anymore.

Jeanne repressed the sigh of frustration that she felt coming on. He could be an infuriating man; she already knew that—though they had met less than twenty-four hours earlier. There was no denying, however, that for the first time in her career she was working with a partner in whom she felt confident. Stuart might have doubts about himself, but she had seen how in times of danger he came through.

Stuart looked up at Jeanne. Something in the tone of her voice and the look on her face made him wonder if she was starting to care about him. One fact he could not avoid was that he sure as hell was starting to care about *her*. He found himself remembering how she had felt in his arms at the way station, when she had slipped him the envelope full of evidence. Of course, her falling into his arms had been just a sham, a way of keeping the envelope safe. That had been Jeanne's only concern. . . . At least, that was what he had thought at the time. Now he was not so sure.

Stuart knew one thing. He felt easier and more comfortable with her than he ever had with a woman. Jeanne was a woman who knew there were risks in life, but she did not let those risks keep her from going ahead with what she had to do.

It was going to be difficult, riding down into the outlaw camp—into danger—with her at his side. The protective feelings that had been growing inside him were even stronger now. But at the same time, if there was going to be a fight, Stuart had an idea that Jeanne Townsend would be a good person to have at his back.

Suddenly, she touched his arm. "Look," she hissed. "I think they're getting ready to pull out."

Stuart raised his head slightly to get a better view and saw that Briggs was on his feet now. One of the other outlaws was putting out the fire with the dregs that were left in the coffeepot. The rest of the men were up and moving around, getting the horses ready to travel again. As Stuart and Jeanne watched, Briggs strode over to Roseanne and Casey and spoke sharply to them, no doubt telling them to get up.

"What are we going to do?" Jeanne asked. "Forrest and Kimbrough aren't here yet."

Stuart glanced over his shoulder, studying the way they had come. "Yes, they are," he said to Jeanne, relief in his voice as in the distance the gambler and the businessman came through the woods, leading the two extra horses.

"We'll have to move fast," Jeanne said as she and Stuart slid down the hill to meet Forrest and Kimbrough. "It looked like Briggs and the others were just about ready to leave."

Stuart nodded grimly. This was going to be their best chance to rescue the two women, more than likely, and he wanted to take advantage of it.

"Did you find them?" Forrest asked as he and Kimbrough reined in.

Stuart nodded. "They're in a little valley on the other side of that hill. You and Kimbrough get up there behind the bushes and be ready to give us covering fire if necessary." He mounted up, Jeanne doing likewise. "We're going in now."

Forrest and Kimbrough nodded in understanding and began to dismount, while Stuart and Jeanne spurred their horses up the hill.

Jeanne could feel her heart beating faster now, and she knew Stuart was feeling the same thing. She made sure her red hair was securely tucked underneath the hat, and then she said to Stuart, "I'm going to ride in hunched over the saddle, so they'll think I've been wounded."

"Good idea. That ought to keep them from recognizing you until it's too late."

The two of them topped the hill and started down the other side, not galloping the horses but not wasting any time getting down into the valley, either. Jeanne bent forward in the saddle, clutching her stomach as if she had been shot there.

As they rode closer, they heard one of the outlaws call out to Matt Briggs, "Hey, boss, it's Telford and Rains!"

Jeanne began to sway in the saddle, and another man exclaimed, "Looks like Rains has been shot!"

Stuart and Jeanne rode right into the clearing. When they were only a few yards from Briggs and the other men, Stuart suddenly jerked back on his reins and brought the horse to an abrupt halt. His Colt seemed to leap out of its holster into his hand, and he lined the barrel on Briggs, who was standing wide-eyed in surprise.

"Hold it!" Stuart barked. "Nobody move!"

Beside him, Jeanne had reined in and pulled the Adams revolver from her holster. She covered the other outlaws, who were standing together in a bunch near the horses. The two kidnapped women had been dragging their feet, and they were still near the edge of the clearing.

Briggs stood stock still, his hand only inches from the butt of his gun; it was apparent that it was taking a supreme effort of will for him not to go for it. Slowly, a smile creased his lean face. "Looks like you meant it when you said you'd remember me, mister," he said mockingly. "Reckon I should have paid more attention."

"Reckon you should have."

Briggs squinted at Jeanne. "Who's that with you?"

"You don't recognize me, Briggs?" Jeanne asked. "You were eager enough to find me at the way station."

An even more shocked look came over Briggs's features. "Goddamn," he said softly. "You were the gal in the black dress. The mousy little one that got knocked out." He glanced at the pistol in her hand. "Be careful with that gun, lady."

Jeanne grinned without taking her eyes off the men she was covering. "I'll be careful, all right, Briggs. I'll make every shot count if you force me to." She lifted her free hand to her head and swept her hat off, letting the waves of red hair tumble free.

Roseanne and Casey were staring openmouthed at Stuart and Jeanne. They had been hoping for some sort of rescue, but they had not really expected it to happen.

Briggs's eyes narrowed. "So those whores were telling the truth," he spat. "You're the one!"

"That's right," Jeanne replied. "I'm the one you were looking for all along. Landreth's not going to be pleased that you had me and let me get away."

"You ain't got away yet. There's only two of you and six of us," Briggs pointed out. "You can't drop all of us."

Stuart inclined his head toward the hill behind them. "Don't be too sure of that. There's two men up there with rifles, and they're pointed right down here at you."

Briggs sneered. "You're trying to run a bluff."

"Find out," Stuart offered quietly. "Go for your gun. Whether I'm bluffing or not, though, you'll be one dead son of a bitch. I'll see to that."

Briggs stared long and hard at Stuart, switched his gaze over to Jeanne for a few seconds, and then growled, "Looks like you've got the upper hand, mister. What do you want?"

Stuart did not believe for an instant that the outlaw was really giving up. He said, "We've come for the women."

Briggs grimaced. "Take 'em. They're no damn good to me." Now that he knew the truth of the matter, he had lost interest in the two prostitutes.

Raising his voice, Stuart called to Roseanne and Casey, "You two get over here. Head on up the hill. There's horses up there for you."

The two women started to hurry past him, but Roseanne paused and looked up at him on his horse. "Thanks, mister," she said.

"Better get moving," he said. "We'll cover you."

Roseanne hurried after Casey. Stuart took his eyes off Briggs just long enough to glance over at Jeanne. She still had the drop on the other outlaws, though her horse seemed to be getting a bit skittish again. The animal had not adjusted well to a different rider; some high-strung brutes were like that.

"All of you unbuckle your gun belts and let them drop easy," Stuart ordered. "Then step away from them. And take it slow."

Briggs frowned as he stared up at Stuart. He was used to reading the danger in a man's eyes, and there was no doubt in his mind that Stuart would shoot him if he had to. Finally he nodded over at his men and said, "Do what he says, boys."

He reached for the buckle of his holster, moving slowly and carefully.

Jeanne's horse suddenly threw its head up and reared, pawing in frenzy at the air with its hooves. Jeanne felt herself slipping from the saddle and had time to cry out before the horse plunged ahead, dumping her. She landed hard, her balance gone.

The horse bolted between Stuart and Briggs, and the gang leader, seeing his chance, yelled, "Blast 'em!" Briggs's hand dove for his gun, snapping it up and firing in a blur of motion.

Stuart's attention was distracted by Jeanne's predicament, but the whine of a slug beside his ear yanked his eyes back to Briggs. He triggered a shot, but Briggs was already moving.

Roseanne and Casey cast terrified glances over their shoulders and began running faster up the hill. On top of the ridge, Forrest cursed and barked at Kimbrough, "Fire!"

Forrest squeezed the trigger of the rifle appropriated from the other dead ambusher, levered, and fired again. Beside him in the brush, Kimbrough began firing with the Henry.

Jeanne knew she had to move. She was too tempting a target sitting on the ground. She rolled a few feet as dust plumes spurted up around her, and then she came up running. She twisted and threw a couple of shots at the gang, scattering them and making them duck for cover.

Cover was something in short supply in the clearing. Stuart's horse was jumping around now, spooked by the gunfire. He hauled down on the reins, trying to bring the animal under control and turn him toward Jeanne. Her horse was running into the woods on the far side of the clearing now, trying to get as far away from the shooting as possible.

If he could scoop Jeanne off the ground and get back up the hill, Stuart thought, they might have a chance. . . .

Just then Jeanne stopped in her tracks as one of the men cut in front of her and lined his gun barrel on her chest. "Hold it right there!" he snarled. "Drop the gun, lady!"

There were too many of them, and Stuart and Jeanne both knew it. As Jeanne hesitated, Briggs sprang forward, looping an arm around her and jerking her in front of him.

The barrel of his gun cracked against her wrist, knocking the revolver from her fingers. Then he jammed his pistol into her side and yelled at Stuart, "Drop it, you bastard!"

Up on the hill, Forrest and Kimbrough both quit firing. They could not shoot now without taking a chance of hitting Stuart or Jeanne. Nearby, Roseanne and Casey had just come over the top of the hill, running and breathing heavily.

Stuart took a deep breath and opened his fist, letting the Colt fall to the ground. There was nothing else he could do—not as long as Briggs was holding Jeanne.

"Come on," Briggs called to his men, starting to back up toward the trees with Jeanne still tightly in his grip. "Get back under cover!"

The men grabbed their horses and hustled them out of the clearing. Briggs jerked his head to indicate that Stuart was to come along, too. Stuart complied, finally getting his horse under control and walking the animal toward the trees.

When they were in the safety of the trees, Briggs mounted up and pulled Jeanne into the saddle in front of him. He laughed and said, "Looks like your plan backfired, lady. I can see why Landreth's so anxious to get his hands on you. He's going to be damn glad to see me."

Jeanne twisted around in the saddle and glared at him. "Listen," she said, "it's me Landreth wants, not this man." She nodded toward Stuart. "Why don't you take me and let him go?"

Stuart started to protest, but Briggs cut him off. "Hell, no. I don't want this hombre on my back trail again. I'd kill him before I'd let him go. But I have a feeling Landreth might like to talk to him first." Waggling his pistol, Briggs indicated two of his followers. "You men stay here for a while and keep their friends pinned down. The rest of us are heading for Taos."

The two men took their rifles and went to the edge of the trees. Crouching behind pine trunks, they opened up with their rifles, peppering the summit of the hill with slugs and making Forrest and Kimbrough hug the ground.

The other three members of the gang swung up into their saddles and spurred their horses into a gallop. Briggs was in the lead, riding double with Jeanne, followed by Stuart. The three outlaws brought up the rear, their guns still out, and Stuart knew they would not hesitate to cut him down if he tried anything. He and Jeanne were caught, and there was nothing they could do about it . . . nothing except wait and see what would happen when they got to Taos.

Chapter Thirteen

George Davis was not the most patient of men under the best circumstances. And waiting for his son to return from hunting down a bunch of murdering kidnappers was enough to make his mind more than a little frazzled.

He was standing in the doorway of the stage station when Marjorie Kimbrough came up behind him and said, "I think Fred's going to be all right, Mr. Davis. He keeps wanting to get up, but I won't let him."

From the cot in the corner of the room, Fred Barker yelled, "George, tell this little hellion I don't need a damn nurse!"

George sucked on his gums as he turned away from the door. "Mind your tongue, boy," he told Fred. "There's a lady present, even if it is a bossy little gal."

Marjorie put her hands on her hips and glared at the crotchety stationmaster. "I'm just trying to take care of Fred, Mr. Davis. He *was* shot last night, you know."

"I know, missy. I ain't forgot."

George doubted that he would ever forget what had happened here. It was nearly noon now, but even in the brightness of day, the memories of the night before were all too vivid.

Arlo Jenks had been his friend, and now Arlo was in the ground, buried under the pines behind the station. George had dug the grave as soon as it was light enough to see, while Marjorie kept an eye on Fred. The young guard had still been unconscious at that time, but he had woken up not long after, and since then it had been a struggle to keep him down.

George had to admit that Fred did not seem injured too badly. He was a young, strong boy, and so far there was no sign of infection. The bullet-plowed furrow in his side would make him stiff and sore for a few days, but he would bounce back quickly from that.

All morning George had listened to the two young people fussing at each other, and he had seen the look in Marjorie's eyes when she spooned the broth she had made into Fred's mouth. All of her maternal instincts were coming to the fore, and unless George missed his guess, some other feelings were cropping up, too. Fred Barker was a handsome young fellow, so it was natural enough that Marjorie would develop a crush on him.

Fred was alternately angered and embarrassed by the whole situation. There was a thin blanket spread over his lower body, but his torso was bare except for the bandages that George had wrapped tightly around him. Fred's protests that he could take care of himself did not do anything to deter Marjorie.

There was another northbound stage due in that evening, and George had already made up his mind to be on it; he was not going to sit around here doing nothing, no matter what Stuart had told him. If his son had not returned by the time the stage arrived, he was going to ride it to Taos and see if he could catch up to him.

Marjorie left off her arguing with Fred for the moment and came over to speak to George. "Do you think they've found Roseanne and Casey yet, Mr. Davis?" she asked.

"Hard to say. Reckon they might've."

"I wish they'd come back." Marjorie's voice dropped. "I . . . I'm worried about my pa."

George had been under the impression that the teenager was more concerned with the two prostitutes than she was with her father, and now he wondered if perhaps he had been judging her too harshly. Her expression showed honest worry, and most of it seemed to be over Benjamin Kimbrough.

Through the open door, George heard the faint peal of a horn. "That's a coach," George said in surprise, since it was still before lunch and the southbound coach was not due until late afternoon and the northbound at supper-time. "Sounds like Linc Woolrich on the box." He knew most of the drivers by the way they blew the dented horns that gave warning of their arrival.

Fred sat up on the cot and swung his legs off the side, wrapping the blanket around himself as he stood and listened to the horn sounding again. "It's coming from the south. Must be an extra run," he said, acknowledging the fact that the stage line sometimes added an extra coach when there was sufficient demand.

Fred hobbled a few steps toward George and said, "Now, dammit, George, I want my pants back! I'm heading on into Taos on that stage to let the sheriff know what's happened."

"No, you ain't," George replied. " 'Cause I'm goin'. Me and the gal will go on and see if we can find Stuart and them others." The decision was made on the spur of the moment, but it seemed to make sense to George. He could not sit around and do nothing anymore, and he knew Marjorie was worried about her father.

"But what about Fred?" Marjorie protested. "Somebody has to stay and take care of him."

"Fred ain't hurt too bad. He'll be all right here until we can send somebody out from Taos to look after him and the station. Matter of fact, with your stage not arrivin' in Taos this morning, they'll probably already've sent someone out."

"But—" Marjorie began.

" 'Sides, it wouldn't be fittin' for a little gal like you and a young feller like him to stay out here all by your lonesome."

"That's right," Fred added quickly, looking somewhat relieved that he would not be left alone with her. "It wouldn't be fitting, Marjorie, and you know it."

Marjorie sighed with a feminine exasperation beyond her years. "I don't have any choice, do I?"

"Don't 'pear that you do," George told her.

The stage rolled into the yard of the station five minutes later. Leathery old Linc Woolrich was at the reins, as George had said, and the guard was a burly young man named Reynolds. George raised a hand in greeting as the cloud of dust raised by the hooves of the horses began to blow away. "Howdy, Linc," he called.

"Howdy, yourself," Woolrich replied. "How come you ain't got a fresh team ready?" He was grinning because he knew only too well that his arrival had been unexpected.

George cursed and then said, "Don't think I couldn't smell you comin' for the past half hour. But there's been quite a ruckus out here, and I just didn't have the time." He glanced toward the dark interior of the coach. "Too many passengers for the regular run? Or were these folks just too anxious to be on their way?"

Woolrich dropped down from the box and lowered his voice. "We only got two passengers, but they're special ones, so hold your tongue."

George frowned, wondering what Woolrich was talking about, when the door to the coach swung open and a young man in a suit climbed out. He was thin and rather pale skinned, as if he spent most of his time indoors. He was followed by another man, also in a conservatively cut dark suit.

The second man was a contrast to the thin, pallid one. Unlike his companion, this man had a ruddy complexion and carried himself with an erect, graceful bearing. He had a short beard and graying brown hair, and his eyes were quick and alert. He strode over to George and Woolrich and asked in a deep, commanding voice, "Will we be stopping here long, Linc?"

"No, sir, Governor, just long enough to change teams," Woolrich said. "We'll get busy."

General Lew Wallace, governor of the Territory of New Mexico, waved a hand casually. "No hurry. My business associates aren't expecting me in Taos until this evening."

"We'll be there on time, Governor, I promise you."

As they went to the corral, George looked back at the two passengers and hissed to Woolrich, "That's Wallace, ain't it?"

"Himself," the driver answered. "The little feller's his secretary."

"Why's the territorial governor on his way to Taos?"

"That ain't none of our business. I've heard that he's got an interest in some mining claims up in that part of the country, though. Reckon he's going to take care of some business."

George glanced thoughtfully at the coach again. "You think he'd mind a little company?"

"What the hell you talking about?"

"I want to ride on into Taos with you. Got a lot to report to the stage line and the sheriff."

"And I suppose it's got something to do with that coach sitting over there," Woolrich commented, pointing at the stagecoach sitting beside the corral.

George nodded, and as the two men worked at changing the teams, he explained what had happened at the station the night before. When he was done, Woolrich exclaimed, "None of that makes a lick of sense! And here's another mystery. You remember that old coot Micah Donahue? He ran a station this side of Albuquerque."

George nodded. "Yeah."

"According to his wife, a gang of murdering skunks came through there looking for a gal. They killed Micah."

"Probably the same gang my son's after. You know I ain't goin' to sit around waitin' for somebody to come along to figger it out for me. I'm goin' to find Stuart."

"You don't know he went to Taos," Woolrich pointed out.

"I don't know he didn't. He was headed that way when he left with them other folks."

Woolrich shrugged. "If you want to ask the governor to share a coach with you, I ain't going to stop you. But don't blame me when he tells you to go to hell."

George approached Wallace hesitantly, taking off his notched and battered old hat as he came up to the governor. "Beggin' your pardon, your honor, sir," George began.

"Yes, sir, can I help you?" Wallace asked heartily.

"Well, sir, we've had a little trouble, and me and a little gal what's in the station need to get on into Taos, and I was wonderin' if you'd mind . . ."

"Sharing my coach?" Wallace glanced at his secretary, who frowned and blanched slightly at the prospect. That could have been the reason Wallace smiled and said, "Of course not, sir. I'm sorry to hear you've had trouble, but I'd be pleased to share the coach with you and the young lady. I'm just glad you're letting me share it with you. After all, I'm just another paying customer!"

George smiled back at him, grinning his near-toothless grin. "Thank you, Governor. I reckon it could be one of them matters of life and death."

"Then by all means, fetch the young lady and we'll get the stage rolling again."

George went into the station and came back out a moment later with Marjorie. Somehow, Fred Barker had managed to get his pants back on, so he was able to follow without too big a loss of dignity. He seemed a little stiff but not in too much pain.

Going to the box, George held out his hand to Reynolds, the shotgun guard. "Gimme that shotgun," he told the young man. "You and Fred can stay on here at the station and look out for the place. I'll ride shotgun."

Reynolds looked to Woolrich for instructions, and the driver nodded to him. "I don't mind riding with George on the box," he said. "We'll send somebody out from Taos to relieve you two boys."

Marjorie was looking somewhat suspiciously at the two men in suits, so George said, "Gal, this here is Governor Lew Wallace and a feller who works for him."

Marjorie's mouth opened. "The governor?"

"That's right, my dear," Wallace said to her. "Here, let me assist you into the coach. Are you interested in literature at all? I recently wrote a novel about the early days of Christianity. It's called *Ben-Hur*."

As Matt Briggs and his three remaining men led their prisoners toward Taos, Stuart glanced over at Jeanne Townsend, who was riding double on Briggs's horse. Her face was expressionless as she rode, but Stuart knew she had to be seething with anger. No doubt she blamed herself for their capture, but that was not fair, Stuart thought. It had just been damned bad luck. . . . A lot like a day a few months earlier, when he had taken a bullet in the arm and his best friend had died.

If nothing else, meeting Jeanne had forced him to think about what had happened to him and about what he had been doing to himself. The sorrow was still there when he thought about Corey Moss, but he was beginning to realize that he must put the past behind him and get on with his life. That is, if he managed to live out the day and figured a way out of this predicament.

He had given a lot of thought to making a break on his own and going for help, but he was flanked by Briggs and another man, with the other two outlaws riding close behind. If he tried anything, he would be cut down immediately. And there was a chance Jeanne might be killed, too. All he could do was wait for the odds to change.

Jeanne was doing the same thing. This was the worst spot she had been in since beginning her career as a Pinkerton operative. The envelope containing the evidence against Landreth was still inside her shirt, and she wished she had had a chance to send it on ahead to the Denver office. At least that way it eventually would have gotten into the right hands.

They had been climbing steadily for several hours, their route taking them up onto the broad plateau where Taos was located. Soon the buildings of the town became visible. As they reached the outskirts, Briggs leaned forward and said, "You're smart enough to know not to raise a ruckus, lady. That'll just get you and your friend dead real quick."

Jeanne shot a glance back at the outlaw leader. "You'd risk a shooting in town?"

"I'll do whatever it takes," Briggs said flatly, and Jeanne could tell that he meant it. That was just one more indication that she had stumbled onto something important.

She was not giving up yet. Somehow she would find a way to stop Landreth.

Taos was a bustling community with plenty of traffic on the streets. Its people were a mixture of whites, Indians, and Mexicans, its businesses designed to serve the ranches and mines in the area. Taos was the center of trade for this part of the territory, and it showed.

Stuart and Jeanne exchanged a look as they rode down the street. They were both highly aware of the threat posed by Briggs and his men. None of the outlaws had their guns out, but they could draw the weapons fast enough. Stuart did not want a shoot-out on the main street of this busy town, and neither did Jeanne.

"Over there," Briggs said quietly, jerking his head toward a hotel up ahead on their left. It was a large frame building with two stories and an ornate façade that made it appear even more imposing. Briggs turned his horse sharply in that direction, crowding Stuart's mount and making the animal dance around for a moment.

"Down the alley," Briggs ordered. The group rode into the dusty alley that ran beside the hotel. At the rear corner of the building was an outside staircase that led up to a second-floor back entrance. Briggs reined in beside the staircase and motioned for Stuart and Jeanne to dismount.

They swung down from their saddles, and one of the other men took the reins from Stuart. Another man also dismounted, and as he moved over beside Stuart and Jeanne, he slid his gun out of its holster and brandished it openly.

Briggs also had his gun in hand as he dismounted. He said, "All right, we're going upstairs. I don't want either one of you trying anything, understand?"

"We understand," Stuart said grimly.

Briggs gave a short laugh. "You'd love to, wouldn't you? I can see it in your eyes. Forget it and you'll live longer."

With Briggs and the other outlaw close behind them, Stuart and Jeanne started up the stairs. For a second, Stuart considered turning and diving back down at Briggs, but then he discarded the idea. He was not sure why Briggs had brought him along in the first place, rather than killing him outright, but he knew the man would not hesitate to shoot.

The door at the top of the stairs opened into a hallway with doors on both sides. With Briggs's gun prodding him in the back, Stuart went down the corridor, walking slowly until Briggs said, "That's far enough."

There was a door on their left, and Briggs reached out with his free hand and knocked on it. A muffled voice asked, "Who's out there?"

Jeanne recognized the voice, even through the door.

"It's Matt," Briggs answered, his tones low.

The door swung open, and the man inside stepped

back quickly, bringing a small pistol up in case someone was trying to trick him. Briggs gave Jeanne a shove that sent her stumbling into the room, and then he jabbed Stuart in the back with the gun and forced him through the doorway. Then he told the other outlaw to wait in the hall, and he followed them inside.

A smile creased Darryl Landreth's face as he exclaimed, "Jeanne! How nice to see you again." His eyebrows lifted as he went on, "I must say you look beautiful, even in that rather bizarre outfit."

"She took the clothes off one of my men," Briggs said as he closed the door behind them. "Reckon he's dead now."

Landreth was staring narrowly at Stuart. "And who's this?"

Stuart spoke up before Briggs could answer. "My name is Stuart Davis," he said. "And I'm a deputy United States marshal. You're under arrest, Landreth." He had guessed who Landreth was, and he had not officially resigned as a marshal yet, so that part of his statement was not a lie.

But it was bravado, under the circumstances, and Stuart damn well knew it.

Landreth laughed heartily. "Under arrest, am I? Well, Marshal Davis, we'll just see about that." The smile dropped off his face as he turned to Briggs and said, "Why did you bring him?"

"Thought he might make a good hostage if we ran into any trouble," Briggs replied. "Besides, the woman here seems to like him, and I thought he might be useful if you needed to make her talk."

Landreth swung his gaze back to Jeanne. "Is that true, Jeanne? Have you gone sweet on this man?"

"That's none of your damn business," Jeanne grated. She wished Stuart had not announced his true identity so brazenly. The knowledge that he was a marshal made it that much more unlikely that Landreth would spare his life.

It did not matter, however, and she knew it. Landreth was going to kill both of them. He had no other choice.

The saloon owner stepped closer to her, lifting a hand

to cup her chin. "You really shouldn't have run away from me like that, Jeanne," he said softly. "I was very upset with you. I was even more disappointed that things didn't work out between us. I had wonderful plans for you."

Jeanne's lips tightened. Her every instinct urged her to spit in the man's face, but that would not serve any purpose. She had to assume there was still a way out of this and ignore the lust she could see in Landreth's eyes.

"Everything still going according to plan?" Briggs asked.

Landreth nodded. "I've received information confirming that the governor left Santa Fe this morning on the stage, just as scheduled. Our man inside the territorial capitol has proven to be reliable. Wallace should be here in less than an hour."

Briggs grinned evilly. "I'm looking forward to this."

Jeanne could feel the blood pounding harder in her head as she suddenly realized what Landreth and Briggs were planning. Her training and experience as a detective had set the deductive process in motion. It all tied together, the letters from the former official, the presence of Landreth and Briggs in Taos today, the desperation with which Landreth had sought to have her captured. . . .

She knew what was going to happen, all right: They were going to attempt to assassinate the governor. And that knowledge did not put her one step closer to stopping it.

Landreth was still holding her chin. He brought up the gun in his other hand and let the barrel trace an aimless pattern down her throat. Beside her, Jeanne sensed Stuart tensing, and she prayed that he would keep his anger under control. Trying some kind of grandstand play now would just get them killed.

"You read the letters you took from my desk, didn't you, dear?" Landreth asked. "You've figured out what we're talking about."

Jeanne stared wide-eyed at him, not having to feign fear.

"You never said anything about her having letters," Briggs spoke up. "If I'd known, I could have searched her for them and brought her luggage. I thought you wanted her because of what she knows."

"I don't know anything," she lied desperately. "I . . . I was looking for money in your desk, I admit that. I'm sorry!" She let her voice break. "I d-don't know why you're doing this to me!"

"Give it up, Jeanne," Landreth advised coolly. "It's not going to work." He laughed and roughly shoved her face to the side, and then stepped away from her. "It doesn't matter. You can't hurt me now, Jeanne. There's not a damn thing you can do now that you're in my hands." Landreth glanced over at Briggs. "You'll be in the plaza when the stagecoach arrives?"

Briggs nodded. "I'll have a clear shot, don't worry. Wallace is already a dead man. He just doesn't know it yet."

Stuart had been frowning in concentration, trying to make some sense of the conversation. The mental effort kept his mind off the rage that was blazing inside him— and helped to keep him from jumping Landreth.

That was what he wanted most, to get his hands on the man from Albuquerque and pay him back for all the evil he had done, all the things he had tried to do.

Now, as Briggs made his arrogant statement, Stuart's brain made the same connections that Jeanne's had a moment earlier. Before he could stop it, an exclamation was jolted out of him by the realization: "You're going to kill the governor!"

Landreth smiled cruelly at him. "That's right, Marshal. We've been well paid to remove General Wallace from office . . . permanently."

"That politician down in Santa Fe, the one who wrote you those letters—he's behind it."

"So both of you read the letters," Landreth said. "Well, you're right. And he's going to continue to pay. He just doesn't know it yet."

Jeanne understood what Landreth meant. "You can't blackmail him without the letters," she pointed out.

Landreth glanced back at her and said, "Oh, so you finally admit you took them."

"No point in not admitting it," Jeanne replied. "You won't get away with it, you know. I've already wired the Pinkerton office in Denver about your plans. You'd better just give it up while you've still got a chance to get away."

Landreth shook his head and laughed softly. "The Pinkerton Agency. Come now, Jeanne, you're still lying. You didn't know until just now what I'm planning. Besides, there is no evidence to connect me with General Wallace's killing. I've taken great pains to assure that. There are only two people who know about it besides Briggs, my politician friend, and myself. And you two won't be doing any talking."

"What about the letters themselves?"

Jeanne's question made Landreth nod thoughtfully. "I suppose I should have them back now. As you so astutely observed, I can't use them to blackmail my client if I don't have them, although I suppose I could bluff him if I had to. Still, things will be much simpler if you just hand them over."

Jeanne smiled. "I don't have them."

Stuart had been watching, his admiration growing as he saw how Jeanne stood up to Landreth. She was calm and collected, as if their lives and the life of the territorial governor did not depend on them getting out of this spot. It was no wonder she had turned into a top operative for Allan Pinkerton, he thought fleetingly. She was good, damned good.

Landreth's features tightened angrily at her cool reply. "It won't do you any good to lie," he said harshly. "I don't believe you."

"It's the truth," Jeanne insisted. "I mailed them to Denver. To the Pinkerton Agency."

For an instant, Landreth looked shaken, but then his smug self-assurance came back. "You wouldn't have done that," he said. "You and I are too much alike, Jeanne. We both think we can handle anything that comes up. Only I'm right and you're wrong. No, you still have those letters, and I suppose I'll just have to search you for them." He smiled. "It should be a pleasant experience."

Stuart could not stop himself when he saw the leer on Landreth's face. His hands formed fists, and he took a step forward. Landreth pivoted smoothly toward him and raised the little pistol, and there was a loud click as Briggs cocked his gun.

Jeanne put a hand on Stuart's arm and said, "No,

Stuart, don't!" Her voice was low but intense. He tore his angry gaze away from Landreth and glanced at her. She shook her head and said softly, "It's all right. It's nothing to get killed over."

Stuart took a deep, ragged breath and forced his muscles to relax.

"That's being smart," Landreth told him. "Of course, it won't make any difference in the long run, but why not prolong life for as long as you can, right?"

Stuart said nothing. He did not trust himself to talk right at the moment.

Landreth stepped back and slipped a watch out of his pocket. He opened it and studied the face for a moment, then looked up at Briggs. "The stage should be pulling in soon. You'd better go attend to our business, Matt. I'll see you back in Albuquerque in two weeks."

Briggs nodded. "You be sure and have the rest of my money when you do."

"You just take care of your end," Landreth told him brusquely.

"I don't miss," Briggs said with a cocky grin. "You know that, Landreth." He opened the door and called the outlaw into the room. Holstering his gun, he said to the other man, "You stay here and do whatever the boss tells you, Barcroft."

The man drew his gun and nodded in agreement. "You bet, Matt."

Briggs slipped out of the room, closing the door quietly behind him.

Landreth turned back to Jeanne. "Now that we have some time," he said, "I suppose we should deal with the matter of those missing letters."

"I'm warning you, mister," Stuart growled. "Keep your goddamn hands off of her!"

Landreth sighed. "This is getting tiresome. Barcroft, take the marshal here down the hall. Three doors down, you'll find another room where some of our associates are waiting. You can turn him over to them."

"What're they supposed to do with him?" Barcroft asked.

Landreth grinned. "I'd say that's up to them. Just be sure to inform them that he's a marshal."

Stuart knew what that meant, and so did Jeanne. He was on his way to his death.

"When you've done that, come back here," Landreth went on. "I may need help with my little job."

Barcroft ran hungry eyes over Jeanne's body and licked dry lips. "I'll be right back," he said hoarsely. He reached out to grab Stuart's arm. "Come on, you!"

Stuart knew he could not leave Jeanne here. If they were split up, it would be the end for both of them. The odds would never be better than they were right now—

Stuart moved quickly, grabbing Barcroft's arm and swinging the man around and then shoving him toward Landreth. He heard Jeanne cry out, "Stuart! No!" The gun in Barcroft's hand was turning toward him. Stuart flung himself forward, reaching out for the weapon.

Landreth shoved the outlaw aside and lashed out with his own gun. Stuart staggered, off balance now, his feet tangled with Barcroft's. The barrel of Landreth's pistol cracked against his temple, knocking his hat spinning and sending brilliant darts of pain cascading behind his eyes. Stuart felt himself falling but could not stop himself.

Jeanne started to leap forward as Stuart collapsed, but she found herself staring down the muzzle of Landreth's gun. "Hold it!" Landreth snarled. "I don't want to kill you yet, Jeanne, but I will if I have to."

Jeanne went down on one knee beside Stuart and reached out to touch his head. The blow from Landreth's gun had opened up a gash in his scalp. Blood from it welled up and then trickled over Jeanne's fingers.

"Touching," Landreth said. "Now get him out of here, Barcroft, and don't waste any time getting back." His gaze was icy as he looked down at Jeanne. "We're not through here. Not by a long shot."

Chapter Fourteen

Marjorie Kimbrough was saying, "But what happens to Ben Hur after that, General?" when the stagecoach rocked to an abrupt halt.

Up on the box, Linc Woolrich had hauled back on the brake and reined in the team when he saw the four people ride out of the woods and onto the stage road. The riders were a good fifty yards ahead of the coach and did not look threatening, but it did not pay to take chances.

Beside Woolrich, George Davis suddenly sat up straighter and lifted the shotgun. He leaned forward, squinted, and then exclaimed, "It's them, by gum!"

As the four people on horseback came closer, riding with shoulders slumped from exhaustion, George felt his spirits sink. There should have been six riders, not four. The two women were in the lead, followed by Lloyd Forrest and Benjamin Kimbrough.

There was no sign of Stuart or Jeanne.

General Wallace's secretary stuck his head out one of the coach windows and called up, "Excuse me, driver, but what seems to be happening?"

Woolrich spat into the dust of the road. "Riders coming," he said shortly.

"I know 'em, Linc," George said. "They ain't out to cause us trouble." He clambered down from the box, taking the shotgun with him, and hurried forward to meet them.

As they rode up, Forrest lifted a hand in greeting. Kimbrough had his head down, and it was obvious he was utterly drained. Roseanne and Casey, despite being somewhat disheveled, appeared to be unhurt and in relatively good spirits.

Kimbrough rode on past George toward the stage. Marjorie saw him coming and popped out of the coach door, running forward to greet her father happily.

"Oh, Daddy, I'm so proud of you!" she shouted as he dismounted and she threw her arms around him.

"You are?" he muttered, and he lifted his head a little higher, suddenly looking far less exhausted.

"Of course! I was so worried about you!" She hugged him tighter and kissed his cheek.

Kimbrough pushed her away slightly so that he could look in her eyes. "But I thought it was Roseanne and Casey you were—"

"Of course I was worried about them. But they're just friends. You're my father!" She hugged him close again, and he began to smile.

Nearby, George Davis came up to Lloyd Forrest and without preamble asked, "What in tarnation happened? Where's my boy and that other gal?"

"I'm afraid the outlaws captured them, sir," Forrest said, leaning on the pommel of his saddle. "Your son and the lady were successful in rescuing Roseanne and Casey here, but the kidnappers managed to get the drop on them."

"Where were you and Kimbrough?"

"We were on a ridge above the outlaws' camp." Forrest swung down from the saddle and stretched his weary muscles. "We were supposed to give them covering fire, and we did manage to help with the escape. There was nothing we could do to help Stuart and Jeanne, though. We were pinned down by rifle fire from some of the outlaws."

"If you was pinned down, how'd you manage to get away?" George asked sharply. He knew he sounded rude and suspicious, but right now he did not give a damn.

Forrest did not take offense. He explained patiently, "Like I said, we were at the top of a ridge. We couldn't go forward, but there was nothing to stop us from retreating once Roseanne and Casey had joined us. We had already found some extra horses for them."

Forrest explained about the ambush and the plan Jeanne had come up with. George listened, becoming more worried as he heard how Stuart and Jeanne had been taken captive.

"There didn't seem to be anything else we could do," Forrest said. "Kimbrough and I wouldn't have been able to track them. We're hardly what you'd call wilderness fighters. Once we had the women, we decided to cut east. I thought we'd hit the stage road sooner or later."

George rubbed his bearded jaw. "Headed toward Taos, eh? Well, that's where we're goin'." He jerked his head toward the coach. "Got a special passenger."

General Wallace and his secretary had gotten out of the stage to see what was going on. They had witnessed the happy reunion of Kimbrough and Marjorie, but they were unprepared for Roseanne and Casey, who immediately brightened up when they saw that there were two well-dressed, unattached male passengers. Old habits were hard to break.

"Howdy, mister," Casey said to Wallace, giving him a smile as she walked past him toward the coach. The sway of her hips was a bit less pronounced than usual, but it was definitely there. Roseanne turned her smile toward the governor's secretary, who began to blush as she spoke to him.

"I hope you two fine gentlemen don't object to us sharing this coach with you," she said. "We've been through a terrible ordeal, and it would be such a comfort to share the company of men of breeding for a change."

"Madam, the governor and I are both married men!" the secretary said stiffly.

Roseanne and Casey looked at each other, and Casey whispered, "The governor?"

When Forrest echoed that question aloud, Wallace nodded. "That's right, gentlemen," he said. "I'm General Lew Wallace, and I'd be happy to have you share this coach with us." He looked at Forrest. "I couldn't help but overhear some of your story, sir. It certainly sounds as if you've been through quite a bit."

Linc Woolrich spoke up. "Tie them horses to the back of the coach and we'll get rolling again. We still got a schedule to keep, you know."

Wallace stepped back and made a sweeping gesture with his right hand. "Ladies," he said, drawing a short laugh from the two prostitutes. They climbed aboard the coach, followed by Kimbrough, Marjorie, Forrest, and the secretary. Wallace was the last one aboard, and he called out to Woolrich, "We're ready, sir."

Woolrich and George were back up on the box now, and with a crack of his whip the leathery driver got the team moving again. With the four horses tied on and trailing behind it, the stagecoach rolled down the trail toward Taos.

As Barcroft hauled the unconscious Stuart out of the hotel room and down the corridor, Jeanne felt like giving up for the first time in her career. It looked as though she had reached the end of the trail. Landreth was not only going to go unpunished for all his other crimes, but he was also going to get away with having the territorial governor assassinated.

Jeanne's head was down. There was nothing she could do.

Landreth stepped closer to her, holding his gun negligently. "We'd better get on with that search now," he said coldly.

Jeanne was still on her knees where she had knelt beside Stuart. She took a deep breath, and a strange thing happened, almost without her realizing it. Her spine seemed to stiffen with resolve, and something inside her cried in protest.

Landreth was not going to win. He *was not*!

Jeanne lifted her head. A slow smile played over her lips. "You don't have to search me," she said softly. With a lithe motion, she was on her feet again, her fingers working with the buttons of the borrowed shirt. She undid two of them and reached inside the garment, making it fall open enough to reveal a sloping expanse of smooth white skin. Her fingers closed on the envelope and drew it out. Extending it toward Landreth, she said, "This is what you want."

"You're right," he agreed, but he was not looking at the envelope, though he reached out with his free hand to take it.

Still smiling, Jeanne lashed out with her foot.

The toe of her boot cracked into Landreth's wrist, sending the pistol spinning away. Before he could react, Jeanne had spun around, gathering strength and momentum and launching another kick. Her foot thudded into Landreth's jaw, driving his head around sharply. All he had time to do was grunt in pain before he collapsed on the floor, out cold.

Jeanne's palms slapped the boards of the floor as she caught her balance and kept herself from falling in the follow-through of the kick. She straightened up, breathing rather heavily for a moment. In her training, she had become acquainted with the French form of combat known as *savate*, and it had certainly proven effective. Landreth had surely expected her to try to get away, but he probably had not expected her to kick him in the head.

She bent over, scooping the fallen pistol from the floor. A footstep sounded in the hall outside, and she knew it had to be Barcroft returning. She darted behind the door just as it started to open.

Barcroft took one step inside the room and then stopped in his tracks as he spotted Landreth's sprawled body. He said, "What the hell!"

Jeanne pressed the barrel of the pistol against his skull just behind his right ear. "Don't move and you won't die . . . yet," she told him as she pulled the revolver from his holster and stuck it in her waistband.

Barcroft stiffened. Jeanne's voice was just about as cold and hard as the ring of metal pressing against his skin. He swallowed nervously and asked, "What do you want, lady?"

"The man you took down the hall. Is he all right?"

"He . . . he was waking up when I left him. Seemed okay, just stunned a little."

"How many men are down there in that other room?"

"Just two," Barcroft answered, eager to keep Jeanne talking instead of shooting.

"All right. We're going down the hall, and when we get there, you're going to tell the men inside to bring Stuart back out. Tell them that Landreth wants to see him again. You understand?"

"Yeah, I . . . I understand." Barcroft's voice was shaky. There was nothing in the world more frightening, as far as he was concerned, than a crazy woman with a gun.

Jeanne took the pistol away from his head as they stepped out into the hall. "Don't get any ideas," she warned him. "I can still put a bullet through your brain if you try anything."

With Jeanne close behind him, Barcroft walked uneasily down the hall. When he reached the other door, he glanced over his shoulder at her, and she nodded curtly, gesturing with the gun. Barcroft sighed and rapped his knuckles on the door.

"Who the hell's that?" came a harsh voice from inside.

"It's me again, boys," Barcroft called out. "Landreth wants to see that goddamn marshal again."

Jeanne heard the key turn in the lock inside the door, and when the panel began to swing open, she was ready. She planted a hand in the middle of Barcroft's back and shoved with unexpected strength. He hit the door and knocked it all the way open, staggering on into the room. Jeanne was right behind him, levering the gun at the shocked outlaws inside. "Don't move!" she ordered.

The men thought about it, she could tell that, but then decided that even though one of them was bound to get her, she would also get one of them. And neither of them wanted to be the one to die.

Stuart was on the bed, one eye already beginning to blacken from the beating they had been giving him. He grinned savagely as he stood up and moved behind the outlaws, taking their guns without ever getting between them and Jeanne. "You made a mistake, boys," he told them, "the same mistake Briggs made."

"They should have killed us right away," Jeanne finished for him.

"That's right." Stuart hefted one of the guns he had taken from the men and then nodded. "This'll do. Drop the belt, mister."

He picked up the holster after the man had unbuckled it and let it fall to the floor. Then he strapped it on and settled the Colt in the holster. Seeing Jeanne was already well armed, he stuffed the second gun behind the holster belt.

"We'd better get them tied up," Jeanne said. "We don't have much time."

"Where's Landreth?" Stuart asked as he began the task of tying up the men with their belts.

"Back in the other room. I knocked him out, but I didn't have a chance to do anything else. And there's no time now. Listen."

Stuart had already heard a child's voice lifting from the street below. "Stage is comin'!" the boy yelled exuberantly. The arrival of a stagecoach was always an event in a frontier town, especially if you were a young boy. "Stage is comin'!"

The words spurred Stuart and Jeanne on. Leaving Barcroft and the other outlaws tied securely in the hotel room, Jeanne locked the door behind her as they went out. Side by side, she and Stuart hurried down the hall toward the staircase that led to the hotel lobby.

If they were not in time, General Lew Wallace was going to die on the dusty streets of Taos.

They pounded down the stairs, drawing startled looks from the hotel guests who were in the lobby. As they burst out through the front door onto the sidewalk, they looked down the street and saw that the coach had already pulled up at the station and come to a stop. Passengers were climbing off through the open door on the side of the coach.

"It's Pa!" Stuart exclaimed, seeing George on the box next to Linc Woolrich. There was no time to wonder about how he had gotten there, or to wonder about Roseanne, Casey, Forrest, and Kimbrough. They were all there, along with Marjorie and a man neither Stuart nor Jeanne recognized.

The last man off the stage was tall and bearded and carried himself with an unmistakable military bearing. Stuart and Jeanne realized who it was in the same instant . . . *Governor Wallace*. They raced across the plaza in a dead run.

Stuart was barely aware of the flicker of late afternoon sunlight on metal from the balcony of a building a block away. But instinct made him palm the Colt from its holster and turn that way as Jeanne lunged forward toward the coach. She hurtled into the governor just as a rifle cracked. Both of them went sprawling to the street as the slug thudded into the side of the coach, sending splinters flying. Stuart snapped off a shot, his eyes spotting Briggs now.

Crouched on the balcony with a Winchester, the outlaw looked just below him at the horse waiting at the hitch rail for a quick getaway. He had been sure that killing the governor would create such an uproar that he could escape in the confusion. But now bullets were humming around his head. Something had gone terribly wrong. When he had seen the woman and the marshal running across the plaza, he had known that he had to move fast, but he had had to wait for Wallace to emerge from the coach.

The people in the street were running for cover now, uncertain where the shots were directed. Women screamed and clutched children to them as they scurried inside.

Jeanne sprang to her feet and held out a hand to Wallace. "Come on, Governor," she urged. "They're after you."

Wallace let her hustle him around behind the coach, where they were joined by the other passengers. George crouched beside one of the wheels, the shotgun in his hands, ready to blast someone. "Get back here, boy!" he called to Stuart. George did not know what the hell was going on, but he saw Stuart standing out in the open, firing at a building down the street.

Stuart saw the flare from the muzzle of Briggs's rifle and felt a burning hand slap at his leg. He staggered, glanced down, and saw the blood on his pants. A bullet had creased his thigh.

Stuart's hand went to his leg as he looked up at the balcony where Briggs was crouched. The outlaw seemed frozen, but only for a moment. Suddenly Briggs vaulted the railing of the balcony, landing heavily in the street below. After he had gained his feet, the outlaw jerked the reins of his horse loose from the hitch rail and pulled himself up into the saddle. He spurred the horse into a gallop.

Stuart saw Briggs coming toward him and knew that

the outlaw intended to ride him down. Briggs levered the Winchester and fired from horseback. Stuart was clutching his wounded leg, trying to stay upright as slugs whipped around him. He straightened, not knowing how many shots were left in his gun, and coolly lifted the weapon. He waited until the sights settled onto the pocket of Briggs's shirt. Then he blew Briggs out of the saddle with the last bullet in the Colt. The outlaw thudded to the street, already dead.

Another gun blasted behind Stuart.

Jeanne jerked her head around to find the new danger and saw Darryl Landreth running across the plaza toward them. He was firing a gun, which Jeanne knew was not his own, since she had it. She could see the crazed look in his eyes. He seemed to know that his plan had collapsed and that there would be no escape for him. His wild expression indicated that if he could have nothing else, he could still have revenge.

With General Wallace standing beside her, she lifted Landreth's gun and fired. The slug took Landreth in the right shoulder, spinning him around. He fell, blood suddenly staining his coat a dark red, and lay still, passed out from the shock of the wound.

"An excellent shot, my dear," General Lew Wallace said as an abrupt silence fell over the street. "Now, will someone tell me just what the devil is going on here?"

George Davis handed the shotgun to Woolrich and ran out into the street to help Stuart. With his son's arm looped over his shoulders for support, George brought Stuart to the sidewalk, gazing proudly from Stuart to Jeanne and then back again. Then he said to Wallace, "Well, offhand, Governor, I'd say these two young folks just saved your bacon."

Epilogue

Stuart's bandaged leg was propped on a stool in front of the chair in the hotel lobby. The pain had just about settled down into a dull ache. He could live with that. The doctor who had treated the gunshot wound had offered to give him something to make him sleep, but Stuart had waved that off. He had wanted to be awake for Jeanne's explanation to Governor Wallace of what had happened here in Taos today.

She had laid out the whole story for the governor, revealing her identity as a Pinkerton agent and starting with her assignment to get evidence against Darryl Landreth. She had filled in the details that Stuart did not know yet, from the accidental discovery of the assassination plot to her escape from Albuquerque with Landreth's men on her trail. When she was finished, Wallace had thanked her again for saving his life and then said, "If you don't mind, my dear, we'll try to keep this whole matter as quiet as possible. We don't want to give anyone else any ideas about the most efficient method of removing me from office."

"That's fine, Governor," Jeanne had told him. "It'll all have to go in my official report to Mr. Pinkerton, but I don't want a lot of publicity, either. That's not good for someone in my line of work."

Now Stuart was thinking about that line of work as he sat alone in the lobby of the hotel. It was late, and most of the lamps were extinguished. The clerk had retreated into his little room behind the desk. There was a fire burning in the fireplace in front of Stuart's chair, taking the chill out of the high-country air. It had been hot this afternoon, but as usual in this part of the country the night was a cool one.

Darryl Landreth was locked up securely in the jail down the street, under heavy guard. His men were there with him—except for Matt Briggs, who was at the undertaker's.

Stuart heard a soft step beside him and looked up to see Jeanne standing there. She wore a blue dress the color of the sky, a dress that had been given to her by Benjamin Kimbrough. Kimbrough had been so glad to reach Taos alive and to have his money belt returned that he had been more than happy to open up his store for anything his companions needed.

The firelight struck glowing highlights off Jeanne's hair. As Stuart gazed up at her, he wondered how he could have ever thought that she was plain looking. That was just more evidence of how good she was at her job.

"Would you like some company?" she asked.

"Yes," he said simply.

She pulled another armchair over beside his and sat down. "I've been talking to Roseanne and Casey. They're going on to Denver, just like they had planned. They wanted to know if I was going to be taking the next stage with them. I told them no."

"You're not?" Stuart frowned. "I thought you had to get back to the Pinkerton office in Denver and turn in your report."

"I've wired enough of the details to them. They can wait a few days for the rest. I want to see how you're doing before I go anywhere."

"I'm fine," Stuart insisted. He gestured toward the bandaged leg. "This was just a scratch."

"Maybe so, but you lost some blood. I don't mind waiting."

Lloyd Forrest strode into the lobby, a thin cigar between his teeth. He nodded to Stuart and Jeanne and said, "How are you feeling, Davis?"

"Not bad," Stuart told him. He glanced at Jeanne. "Not bad at all."

A slight smile made the corners of Forrest's mouth twitch. "I'm not surprised. You have quite a lovely nurse there." He walked to the fireplace and stood in front of it for a moment, hands clenched behind his back. He turned around and leaned an arm on the mantle above the massive stone fireplace. "And we all had quite an adventure," he went on as if he had not paused. "I've enjoyed knowing both of you."

"You're a good man, Forrest. . . ." Stuart said, letting his voice trail off as if he did not know how to continue.

Forrest's smile became more ironic. "Why don't you say the rest of it? I'm a good man, so why am I wasting my life as a gambler? That's what you meant."

"Well?"

"To one extent or another, we are all what we have to be, my friend," Forrest said. He reached inside his jacket and took out the piece of paper that Jeanne had seen him looking at several times in the last couple of days. It was a letter, she saw now, just as she had suspected. "We can try to change," Forrest said softly. "Sometimes we can have the best reason in the world to change. But we are what we have made of ourselves, no more, no less."

He looked down at the letter and thought about the long road he had been on and all the ways his life had changed. Then he glanced up at Jeanne and realized why she had so attracted him in the first place. Though at first she had seemed demure and submissive—qualities that reminded him of Marion Wilson—there was a fire and independent spirit that shined through even then. He smiled as he realized he could never be happy settling down to the life that Marion would map out for him, no matter how tempting the hearth. Though he might yearn for someone to share his life, he knew now that as far as Marion Wilson was concerned, he had made the correct choice fifteen years ago, and it was still the correct choice today. Someday the right woman might come along— perhaps someone like Jeanne Townsend—who shared his wandering spirit and with whom he could make a new life. Until then, he would be content with the life he had created for himself, a life that was not so very bad at all.

Forrest's hand clenched into a fist, crumpling the

paper. With a flick of his wrist, he tossed it into the fire. It flared up for an instant and then was gone.

"Forgive me," he said. "I have been waxing overly philosophic. I bid you good night."

Forrest strode out of the lobby, the cigar at a jaunty angle.

"I don't know whether to feel sorry for him or admire him," Jeanne said.

"All you can do with a man like that is let him go his own way."

Jeanne looked over at Stuart. "What about you? Are you going to go your own way?"

"What do you mean by that?"

"Are you still determined not to go back to being a marshal?"

Stuart did not meet her eyes. He gazed into the fire instead. "That's a part of my life that's over. The things that have happened the last couple of days haven't changed that."

"You are a lawman, Stuart. You're not going to be happy staying at that way station the rest of your life."

"Aren't you taking a lot on yourself, telling me how to live my life?"

"I don't think so," Jeanne said softly. "Seems like after saving it a time or two, I've got a stake in it now."

Stuart could not help but grin. "You have any suggestions about what I should do?"

"As a matter of fact, I do. I told you that Mr. Pinkerton has always wanted me to work with a partner. I think you'd do just fine."

Stuart was already shaking his head before the words were out of her mouth. "I wasn't cut out to be a detective," he insisted.

"You're the most competent man I've ever met." She reached out and laid her hand on top of his. "The only one I've ever trusted. We could work together, Stuart. I know we could."

George Davis cleared his throat as he stepped into the room, his old pipe in his mouth. "Sounds like a smart idea to me, son," he said. "I been tellin' you for a month you wasn't never goin' to be satisfied helpin' out around the station."

"Pa, I'm surprised at you," Stuart said with a grin. "You've been eavesdropping. I thought you couldn't hear, old man."

"Old man, is it?" George bristled. "Reckon I hear what I want to hear. Now I'll leave you two young folks alone, but you listen to that gal, son. She ain't only pretty, she makes a load o' sense, too." He stomped out of the lobby, trailing a cloud of smoke behind him.

"Maybe he's right," Stuart said thoughtfully, looking at Jeanne. "A Pinkerton agent . . . Sounds like it might be pretty interesting."

"We could find out," Jeanne breathed, leaning closer to him, her face only inches away from his now.

"Now that's more like it," George mumbled to himself. Quietly, he closed the door and walked down the sidewalk, breathing in the crisp, cool air. He glanced back at the hotel window and saw the two heads coming together inside, and a broad smile wreathed his whiskery face.

He walked away, muttering about young whippersnappers and grinning from ear to ear.